Being Hansel and Gretel

By: Adam M. Baig, 2013

1

Once upon a time, within the Harz Mountains, surrounded by many forests, in a small house at the outskirts of a small town of Osterwieck, there lived Gundovald Holzhacker, a father and a woodcutter by trade. His house among several others was located just outside the town's protective outer wall. He lived with his wife Hiltrude and their two children, who were brother and sister, and were fraternal twins. Their names were Johannes and Margaretha Holzhacker, but their parents often referred them as simply Hansel and Gretel for short. During the week, Gundovald left for the Harz Mountain woods at dawn with his axe and hand-drawn wagon, then would come back at near dusk with some chopped wood, and would later bring all of his saleable wood to the marketplace of Osterwieck to sell, every Saturday. Then, Gundovald would enjoy a restful Sunday with his family. Osterwieck was located within the Holy Roman Empire of Germany and within the Duchy of Saxony. Hansel and Gretel, the woodcutter's twin children, were born in the spring of 1308, and they both had inherited their mother's blonde hair, leaving the father as the only brunette of the family. The family of four also owned a farmstead, adjacent to their house, and which had a garden of home-raised crops along with a pig sty (having a boar, sow and their piglets) and a chicken house. Being Christians, Gundovald, Hiltrude, Hansel and Gretel attended church, every Sunday in Osterwieck before engaging in some leisurely activities.

Felling dead trees only and chopping wood from either his felled trees or from trees that had recently fallen themselves, Gundovald Holzhacker often worked very long and hard, every weekday, because the family was poor. Having no horse, Gundovald, wearing his hooded wool cloak, hauled his wagon, full of chopped wood, to Osterwieck's marketplace at the center of town himself on the Saturdays. Thankfully, however, he made just enough money, selling his product, there. Also, despite the family's overall impoverished state, the Holzhacker family was happy, loving and caring towards each other, and was sufficiently fed. Gundovald Holzhacker also never failed to provide well enough for his family, and seeing his wife and two kids smile always gave him reasons to keep going.

While Gundovald was out in the woods in the morning, Hiltrude would take her two children out to the garden and chicken house to harvest eggs and crops when permissible. Later, if needed, she would request her two children's assistance in the laundry of their wool overgarments and their linen undergarments at the narrow Ilse River, which also ran through town. Then, she would school Hansel and Gretel until the early afternoon. Afterwards, all three gave themselves freetime until the father would come home in the evening. In their freetime, Hansel and Gretel had their own personal means to keep themselves joyful. Hansel had a toy wooden sword and shield along with a clay knight figurine, while Gretel had some flat tin dolls. They together also had their fabric-stuffed leather ball, which both loved to use for playing catch with each other. All of these would be their only toys, but Hansel and Gretel made the most of what they already had, even if they could not have anymore toys for themselves. Both played games together on a regular basis, and they even played chase with an old discarded wheel to give themselves more amusement. Seeing Hansel and Gretel laugh and play games together always made Gundovald and Hiltrude feel rewarded and happier with themselves as well for the parents loved their children dearly and cared for them a lot. Indeed, to Gundovald and Hiltrude, Hansel and Gretel were a wonderful blessing to them. The Holzhackers also had a cat, which helped rid the farmstead from unwanted rodentian pests, and added itself well to the family. Furthermore, Hiltrude's younger sister, Adalberta, who worked as a spinner in Osterwieck, paid biweekly visits to the Holzhacker household, which added to the family closeness. Adalberta, unfortunately however, had no children of her own and had a drunken and occasionally abusive husband, who did not care to come with her to visit her sister's family. Yet, Hansel and Gretel were always happy to see their aunt Adalberta, and always came running to her when she visited. Adalberta loved to be with them too, and the three would play some games, while her sister and brother-in-law could take a short respite.

2

The Holzhacker family continued their monotonous but satisfactory routine of life, and Hiltrude always let her husband know that he was a wonderful husband and father. She was very affectionate to Gundovald too, and he loved returning his share of it. However, the family happiness would end when Hiltrude, sadly, died from a disease known as ergotism when the twins were five years old. The remaining Holzhackers deeply missed the mother of the family dearly, and Gundovald spent as much time with his children as possible, consoling them. Hansel and Gretel often cried, lamenting the loss of their loving mother, and Gundovald spent hours holding his two children, while trying to fight back his own tears. However, despite having to take the time for deep mourning, Gundovald still had to spend six days per week on his job so that he and his children could continue living. It also certainly would have been what Hiltrude would have wanted for them as well. So, Gundovald took Hansel and Gretel out to the woods with him to help him load his latest newly cut wood. The new responsibilities helped Hansel and Gretel emotionally heal faster, and seeing his two children work helped Gundovald emotionally heal faster as well. Gundovald always complimented Hansel and Gretel for doing exceptional work, which finally brought a smile to their faces again. Yet, it took a while for the three of them to get used to not seeing only their cat and not Hiltrude at home, as the Holzhackers came back from the woods in the evening, however. Though Gundovald knew that his two children felt rewarded for helping him at his job, he also felt that Hansel and Gretel, considering their young age, still needed maternal, nurturing care. This concerned Gundovald a lot, especially seeing Hansel and Gretel easily slip into occasional boredom and despair, while in the woods with him. So, in addition to satisfying his own loneliness, he felt that the right thing to do was remarry and let Hansel and Gretel be properly developed by a new mother figure. Thus, after Sunday Church and while Adalberta watched over Hansel and Gretel, Gundovald set out and decided to express his availability to a single and childless woman, named Eadburga. Gundovald knew Eadburga from town as an acquaintance, and she was very attractive. Eadburga was thrilled to know that Gundovald was available again for she was always secretly interested in him, and sometimes peeked at him from afar, while he sold his chopped firewood at the marketplace on Saturdays. Eadburga knew that she could not do anything to win Gundovald at first, since she knew that he was married, but all that was going to change now. Gundovald and Eadburga almost instantly became a couple, and the courtship lasted only six months, prior to their marriage; but Gundovald hastened the courtship for the whole family's sake, while Eadburga surely let him do it. Hansel, Gretel and Adalberta also found no possible issue with Gundovald's new love, when she met them as well for the first time.

3

With a new mother of the house, the Holzhacker household felt complete again; and Eadburga Holzhacker was kind, loving and very affectionate to her new husband, and he was very happy with her too. However, there actually was one major issue. Eadburga heavily resented Hansel and Gretel, though she fully and successfully kept her resentment of them secret. Eadburga Holzhacker did not want to care for stepchildren for she felt that if she were to care for children at all, then they would have to be either natally hers or be adopted foundlings, but not so if they belonged to one parent and not to her as well. Furthermore, though Gundovald hoped for a while that she could have them, it was found that Eadburga could not have children of her own either. Therefore, she felt that Hansel and Gretel were completely undeserving of her care and absolutely nothing would change her apathetic attitude for them, and she always remained stoic to them when they were any form of distress. Hansel and Gretel were at first open to their stepmother, but the twins quickly learned that she was closed-minded to them. They were a nuisance to their new stepmother, and she was not afraid to show it often. However, just to ensure the peace in the household and the love of her husband that she dearly loved, Eadburga tolerated Hansel and Gretel only when it was important to do so. Examples of these tolerations included preparing meals for them, looking after them during the day, and devoting some time to school them, while their father was out working in the woods. Yet, Hansel and Gretel had their newfound reasons to fear their stepmother for she punished them harshly and severely, even for trivial mischief, all in their father's absence. Though the cat was not allowed to roam outside without supervision or it may escape the farmstead, sometimes Hansel and Gretel would forget to close the door after entering the house. Eadburga raised her voice so loud at them that Hansel and Gretel often unnecessarily kept extra close watch over the cat thereafter. Eadburga schooled Hansel and Gretel in such a non-subtle tone of voice, which easily gave the impression to the twins that they were a burden to her. She often roared at the frightened Hansel and Gretel even if they just nicely asked her for a small extra favor or if they answered incorrectly to one of her questions in her schooling review sessions. Should either Hansel or Gretel do anything wrongly or not fully correctly, demeaning insults would result from their stepmother as well. Despite some passage of time following her marriage to Gundovald, Eadburga still did not want to devote more time than she had to do for her stepchildren. During laundry time, Eadburga was unnecessarily strict to Hansel and Gretel and forced them to take more time than necessary to clean the linen undergarments, while she just sat and watched them. When the twins ran to their father, coming back from the woods with chopped wood, for comfort, their stepmother created a multitude of lies to cover herself. This would result in their father nicely asking his children to comply, while disbelieving Hansel and Gretel's objections to their stepmother's lies. Eadburga continued to treat Gundovald affectionately and always readied him his porridge, pork and melons for dinner, which certainly made it difficult for Hansel and Gretel to expose his new wife's views toward them. Since Gundovald Holzhacker exhaustively continued to work hard almost every day to earn two silver pfennigs that he received each week, so that his family had food on their plate and a roof over their heads, he could not bother to find time to question his new wife's treatment of his children. As long as Hansel and Gretel were healthy and fed and always there to be with him every evening, Gundovald was overall satisfied; and so was Eadburga for her own reasons. Also, though he never admitted it aloud, Gundovald also had some psychological weakness, which further enabled Eadburga to be nasty to his children behind his back, all while making him feel loved and appreciated. This left Hansel and Gretel with no one to help them. It would not be long till Hansel and Gretel no longer played joyfully together without worry and no longer found themselves in the occasional sibling argument for now the twins always had to work hard together to appease their stepmother. The brother and sister learned that all was well enough, so long as Eadburga did not yell at them or insulted them on any given day. Hansel and Gretel could be more playfully themselves when their father was home for the evenings and on Sunday after church, but being their childish selves was overall a far cry from when their real mother was with them. Hansel and Gretel themselves now knew that their stepmother despised them immensely, and they eventually had to learn to be very quiet when she took an occasional nap during the day, so that they would not accidentally disturb her. Eadburga Holzhacker, though still tolerating their presence when need be, only wanted to rid herself of her two stepchildren—her unwanted burden, and then have the peaceful, cozy life with her husband only. She would not, however, dispose of them directly for this would only bring trouble upon her in many ways for she knew that her husband loved them dearly. So, she had to wait for just the right time to implement the right plan to strike. Unfortunately for her, this moment may take a long time to arrive, but once it would, all will be well thereafter. So, she maintained her patience.

4

It was now the spring of 1315 and Hansel and Gretel Holzhacker had continued to put up with their stepmother for two years now. They continuously hoped that their stepmother would change and become more loving and accepting of her stepchildren, but to their ongoing astonishment, absolutely nothing changed. In fact things became worse for Eadburga became increasingly grouchy, moody and even more violent, while still keeping her husband pleased. Of course, Hansel and Gretel would bear the brunt of it, and they still could not do anything to reveal any of this to their father. Hansel and Gretel's seventh birthday went almost without notice from Eadburga, but then suddenly wished them well for that day, when their father brought it up to them. Gundovald Holzhacker still continued to work diligently, dealing with the family's impoverished state, and earning enough money for himself and his family, while hauling and selling his chopped timber. On a typical day, Hansel and Gretel helped their stepmother in their farm, harvesting the eggs, turnips, oats and melons, prior to their schooling. They had to obey her every whim or face punishment as always. Then, Eadburga took an afternoon nap, giving Hansel and Gretel time for themselves. Both still could not play any game outside because it may result in either of them or both laughing out loud in fun. Then, their stepmother would rush out yelling and slapping them for disturbing her nap again. Sometimes a neighborhood boy or girl would come to the Holzhacker stead to ask Eadburga if he or she could play with Hansel or Gretel respectively. However, Eadburga only yelled at the visiting child to never come back here again. Hansel and Gretel could not understand why their stepmother was so cruel, just because another child of their age only kindly asked to play with them. What made matters more difficult was the unexpected numerous rainy days that seemed to ensue without end. So, the fraternal twins had to stay inside during the day, where both could only whisper and play with their toys as quietly as possible, while their stepmother took her afternoon slumber. Boredom often overcame them as Hansel and Gretel only silently watched the rain that continued to fall from their window. Though only a burden to a child, the ongoing rainy days would become a major issue to an adult and to a whole community and perhaps even a whole nation. What astonished everyone including Gundovald and Eadburga, the townspeople of Osterwieck, the citizens of the Holy Roman Empire of Germany, as well as all of the inhabitants of Europe was that there were astonishingly few days where the Sun actually shone now. An unprecedented wet spell had befallen medieval Europe, starting from this spring season of 1315. Hansel and Gretel only thought about their frustration that they could not go outside and play, but unfortunately, a new and more dangerous, frightening and nearly hopeless lifestyle lay in waiting for the seven-year-old fraternal twins. History would remember this awful weather span, which lasted two years, as the Great Famine of 1315-1317. With too much watering of the grounds from the endless rainfall during the spring, and the cool summer that would follow, many crop failures ensued throughout medieval Europe. There were very few yields of grains, fruits and vegetables, comparing to before. With the food availability plummeting, the prices for food rose exponentially; and absolutely no one regardless of status and class was prepared for this. People began to starve, and they increasingly competed for any food to obtain. Crime, involving theft, rose quickly as well within almost all municipalities. With the extremely rainy spring, many cattle and pigs started dying rapidly because the crop failures yielded no straw, hay and vegetables, needed for their fodder. Fresh and edible meat became scarce and very expensive, and if the declining livestock was not enough, salt, which was heavily needed to preserve meat, became rare and expensive as well. This was because the moist air from the rains heavily inhibited evaporation of the water from the salt in the buckets that carried the saltwater from the North and Baltic Seas. A pfennig could purchase a loaf of freshly baked bread prior to 1315. Now, a pfennig could only buy a slice of stale bread, which was often not fully mold-free. With no home-grown crops for themselves, Gundovald Holzhacker now had to work harder, chopping more wood to sell as the family of four became poorer from the dire consequences, while Eadburga continued to take out her anger and frustration on Hansel and Gretel, who now had to hide from her more and more, while Eadburga yelled in frustration, trying to find them. Eadburga, during the day on her few mild moods, brought her stepchildren into the forest to find wild berries and hazelnuts to help keep food on their plates. Though the twins were often drenched, they knew getting anymore food from anywhere would become more and more important.   On days when Hansel and Gretel would find many hazelnuts and berries, their stepmother never once thanked them nor complimented them.   Eadburga yelled at them and called them poor excuses for children on the days when they could not find a single nut or berry, even when they made an honest effort to find any.   Hansel and Gretel were at least getting a little used to Eadburga's never-ending disdain for them, but often the twins sighed and shook their heads behind her back, when Eadburga went on another of her complaints about them.   Otherwise, hiding and sometimes running away from her, while she angrily chased them with clawed hands was the norm.   Hansel and Gretel would not come out of hiding until their father returned home, even if they would have to sit in a dark, muddy area in a copse of trees all day.   Their togetherness maintained their spirits at the very least.   Still however, they wished that their father would know about their stepmother's never-ending nasty nature to them.   Gundovald mentioned to Hansel and Gretel that their Aunt Adalberta would not pay visits to the household anymore because their aunt was increasingly preoccupied with her husband.   In actuality, Eadburga barred their aunt from visits, and Eadburga craftily ensured that her husband would not have any chance to learn of her intentions to his children from the children's aunt, should she stay over and find out anything.   The twins were sad because they missed their aunt but their stepmother only reacted with apathy, anger or even a slap when they brought their aunt up. The decreasing food supplies to satisfy their hungers only worsened their situations.   Yet, Hansel and Gretel felt some reasons to be happy because they still had each other and

14

their father. Also at the very least, woodcutters including Gundovald saw a higher demand for their services for the following fall season was unseasonably cold, and people needed more firewood earlier than usual. Yet, though Gundovald now made four pfennigs per week, it was still overall difficult to maintain enough food for the family with the sharp inflation, but it was still just enough earnings and food to contribute to the family for the most part. At home, there were also no such things as table scraps to Gundovald, Eadburga, Hansel and Gretel. Gundovald and Eadburga had to slaughter more than usual of their piglets to help maintain the food, and that was after many of their piglets had already died of starvation. Their boar and sow were also unhealthily losing weight fast. The Holzhacker cat acted as a wild predator even when hunting a single beetle.

The famine began to result in the deaths of people from Osterwieck and other German towns and cities from starvation, extreme malnutrition and lack of needed proper heat. Along with the population decline, this would also mean that there would be less customers and money for Gundovald's chopped wood, even though he had lowered his price. Gundovald also had to keep his chopped wood more tightly enclosed in the marketplace when he noticed that people started stealing his wood, when he was not looking. The ensuing winter of 1315-1316 was unlike any seen in medieval Europe for up to two centuries. It was totally and incessantly frigid, and many more people died, not just from hunger but also from diseases like pneumonia, which became rampant. Many mothers and fathers had no choice but to

15

watch many of their children die slow and painful deaths from starvation and disease since the children were the most susceptible, and other parents did all they could to give any remaining table scraps to their surviving but weakening children. Many adults were also tempted to keep all the table scraps for themselves to ensure their own survival. Hansel and Gretel now also became increasingly undernourished, and they often could not hide it. In various medieval European municipalities, many grandparents often allowed themselves to starve to death in order to leave more available food to keep their children and grandchildren fed as much as possible. The politically powerful Catholic Church and the political power of Europe's highest monarchs had no power to reverse the immensely devastating weather. Thankfully, the Holzhacker household was kept nice and warm with plenty of firewood, during the freezing days, and Gundovald scrounged to find any hope for any relief from all this, especially when he saw Hansel and Gretel joyfully play together in the evenings amidst their weakened states. Hansel and Gretel for the time being were actually among the luckier children.

5

Indeed, the great economic prosperity, the high population growth, the high crop and livestock yields and the faithfully warm seasons that medieval Europe enjoyed in the 1200s grounded to a halt almost seemingly overnight. The year 1316 would be a very disastrous year for again the spring season was filled with a disproportionate amount of rainy days. Again, next to no crops would grow, and even Holy Roman Emperor and King Friedrich III (the Fair) among other European nobles had to watch his food storage, though the nobles had a good supply of food reserves, which was enough. Many more individuals, whether man or woman, adult or child, from the general populaces continued to suffer from starvation, malnutrition and disease, and died within the early months of 1316. Even adults now struggled to survive; and many who were also parents now felt that they had to do something drastic in order to save themselves. They started abandoning their young children under adolescent age, who now became a burden for the parents and who now suddenly had to fend for themselves. Adults would take their now-unwanted young children to a certain area and leave them there and ordered them to remain there, even if their parents disappeared from sight. These unfortunate children were either made aware or not that they were now abandoned, but all were not allowed to come home, even if they were to find their way. Many abandoned children were often left in the squares of municipalities, and sadly many of these abandoned children simply died of starvation and lack of shelter, but a very few lucky others either were adopted by new and wealthier families who could care for them, or were found by monasteries. Many other abandoned children were led out of the main municipal gates and requested that the guards not let them back inside. These children would then have to head to the forests where they may be able find their own food there, if they were lucky. Eadburga Holzhacker first learned of the practice of child abandonment, when she yapped at three abandoned and wandering demented young stranger children to leave her property or she would strike them with a broom. Diseases such as dysentery, malaria, bronchitis and typhoid fever became rampant, which continued to add to the death tolls and to the weakened states of the survivors in the populaces. Crime also remained high as people, who had no money or far from enough money, continued stealing food and money from others who had it, so that they could survive for at least a little longer. Priests, monks and nuns in their churches and monasteries did their best to feed and care for the starving, the sick, the malnourished and the abandoned, which was most appreciated; but there were many more that needed relief, which was far beyond what the religious faithful could do. Those of the religious life had to ensure their own survival as well, for that matter. Gundovald Holzhacker now carried little chopped firewood to the marketplace. He did not bother bringing a lot of firewood, considering that there were fewer and fewer customers; but now he could oversee his entire sales product, preventing thievery. However, he could not help but occasionally give one piece of firewood to a wretched family—parents and non-abandoned children together—begging on their knees at his stand with flowing tears for the chance to keep themselves warm. Seeing all family members wear a smile when they received one chopped log followed by an extremely heartfelt debt of gratitude gave Gundovald a warm feeling as well. Gundovald was still making some money from his sales, since firewood was still in great demand albeit only from the remaining survivors. He could still buy some more food for his family, regardless of how much food. At home, things were the same as well, unfortunately. Eadburga shamelessly managed to strike an abandoned boy, who was the same age as Hansel and Gretel, with a broom, when she found him scrounging for a single egg in her chicken house. She chased him off, screaming and threatening, while wielding her broom like a sword. The next day, she angrily ordered her stepchildren to bury the same boy, who was found dead, not far from their farmstead. Both fraternal twins certainly suffered several nightmares, following this unwanted experience. In the municipalities, many surviving horses, which were weak from not having enough grass and fodder, were later slaughtered by the starving adults and by starving whole families, who had to resort to newer drastic measures. As the spring dragged into the summer with still too much rain, suppressing the crops, Eadburga had to slaughter all but two hens in the chicken house. She reluctantly gave enough cooked chicken for Hansel and Gretel, while keeping more for herself, not surprisingly. At least Gundovald gave some of his chicken to his children, while Eadburga created false excuses for needing the extra food for herself only. The occasional sunny day had no effect on the Holzhacker household for they knew it would be short-lived. Thus far, thankfully the Holzhackers neither had been so badly starved that they were to begin losing their vital functions nor caught a disease, unlike many who had in Germany already. On another dismal and rainy day, Eadburga yelled and struck a drenched, raggedy, demented and abandoned seven-year-old girl and her little four-year-old sister, when they knocked on her door in tears, crying and begging on their knees at the doorstep for a single scrap to eat. After successfully striking them and chasing them off the farmstead with her broom, Eadburga yelled at them at the top of her lungs to go to the forest to find something, while wielding her broom as usual. Even though Eadburga was suffering undernourishment herself, she always had enough strength to "protect" her farmstead. The next day, Gundovald stumbled upon the same dispersed sisters' lifeless bodies on his route through the forest. With sadness, he said a prayer for them and buried them, and then thanked God for His helping hand on behalf of his own children. Starting to feel the non-ignorable effects of undernourishment, Gundovald now could only chop and haul a small amount of wood for that was for all he had the strength and stamina. Hansel and Gretel on their freetime saw more abandoned children leaving Osterwieck, passing by their farmstead, and heading into the forest in the midst of the rain. With little remaining strength and stamina, all these children could only trudge and some only had the remaining strength to crawl. Hansel and Gretel with their weakened arms hugged each other, while watching them, and dearly hoped and prayed that they would not be next. Gundovald, with his wife and his two children, said a prayer on every evening for relief and thanked God for every night that they could still enjoy their togetherness on Earth. On a night before sleeping, Gundovald, using one hand to help keep his weakening self up, kissed Hansel and Gretel and wished them a good night, and always promised that he would do anything to ensure their survival. Both fraternal twins always replied that they already knew this, but always thanked him as well. Then in his and his wife's own bed, Eadburga with her remaining strength often affectionately threw her arms and one of her legs around Gundovald, snuggled herself to her husband, and in whisper told him how wonderfully he had been handling this whole situation. Gundovald always smiled and embraced back in thankfulness and encouragement, every time she made him feel this good about his competencies. Eadburga never failed to give her husband a lot of affection, which he could never underappreciate.

6

The climate continued to be unkind to medieval Europe as the fall and winter of 1316 were again below-average in temperatures; and the population of medieval Europe noticeably declined further, and there was still no relief in sight. The boar and sow of the Holzhacker farmstead died of extreme malnutrition, and when Gundovald and Eadburga discovered them the next day, they both fell into temporary relief and happiness for they had more to eat for a couple of days, though not for many more days, since they could not preserve the meat for a longer period of time. Hansel and Gretel found this nourishing relief quite comforting and strengthening too, all while both twins did all they could to comfort each other, when one sibling was starting to lose all faith and hope. With numerous surviving livestock and draft animals killed and consumed, very few people, but some people, then resorted to one of the most avoided practices in humanity—cannibalism. Though this involved people survival-cannibalizing only the recently passed, many others balked from this. These others preferred to find any other possible alternative albeit very few or none. The Holzhackers had not once considered survival-cannibalism, even though all were still alive and only very few others were among them—less dead people in their immediate midst—on the outskirts of Osterwieck. Eadburga found cannibalism in general disgusting (thankfully for Hansel and Gretel!), and did not resort to finding dead abandoned children, who were en route to the forest before they fell. Indeed an act against the Judeo-Christian teachings, many more medieval Europeans preferred to bury their dead, rather than cannibalize them; but there were still the very few that would do anything to ensure their own survival.

It was now the spring of 1317, hunger and malnutrition still continued to be rampant, and this time, the Holzhacker household was not spared. Hansel and Gretel's ninth birthday was almost without notice except for one statement by their father before he trudged into the woods with his axe and wagon. This time, Eadburga only ordered them to do her laundry including her long wool dress in the pouring rain, and called that their birthday present from her. Hansel almost threw his stepmother's dress in her face in anger, but Gretel calmed him down and said that doing this for a short time would be better than having to hide outside all day. Hansel obliged. Gundovald's chopped wood became smaller and smaller with his declining strength, and he could now only bring little chopped wood to Osterwieck's marketplace, even with Eadburga's help. While having only a few customers, his very little earnings were now far from enough to support both himself and his family for the cost of food still remained high. He still had his two remaining hens, but he and his wife chose to keep them instead of slaughtering them, since he and his family could at least share two laid individual eggs for roughly every day and a half. The chickens continued to find their own nourishment, such as insects on the ground, as well. Gundovald now began to collapse with exhaustion more frequently in the forest, and he often felt nauseous. He now felt that he was going to be among the next to face starvation because he no longer had the strength to even do any of his work. One night, Gundovald, after wishing Hansel and Gretel a good night and doing all he could to reassure them that all would be well, lay in bed with Eadburga, but all he could do was toss and turn with his lessening strength for increased worries filled his mind. He was getting weaker and weaker, and he had less and less drive and money to keep the family fed, and so he asked his wife for any possible new suggestions about feeding the family with any suffices, even if the potential yield of new food would be very small. Eadburga, however, had formulated a different answer for this was the perfect time for what she had been long awaiting. Now she could finally get rid of her two unwanted stepchildren with any legitimacy. She would forcibly suggest child abandonment that she had been observing. She knew all along that chasing them into the forest herself in Gundovald's absence would not work due to their father's love for them. Gundovald would only immediately set forth into the forest to look for them, and eventually realize his wife's intentions. Thus, Eadburga would therefore bring upon a less blatant plan to abandon them in order to show that she still cared for Hansel and Gretel though untruthfully so. This plan would thus appear to be a reluctant child abandonment, only so that Eadburga and Gundovald would solely survive for the greater good. Thus, without a second thought, Eadburga calmly offered her suggestion, which would be both Gundovald and Eadburga leading Hansel and Gretel deep into the forest with only a piece of bread for each of them. Once deep into the forest

24

enough, the adults would then light a campfire for them, and then leave them there; and the children would have no choice but to fend for themselves, since they would not be able to find their way back. Then, while Gundovald stared at his wife with bewilderment, Eadburga then calmly mentioned that she and Gundovald will at last be alone and happy, having just enough food and money and all the love and comfort for themselves only. Gundovald, still slightly shocked, replied with an absolute no, despite his love for Eadburga. He then stressed that Hansel and Gretel would never survive on their own in the forests, and they would be being targets for wild predators. He then recalled his encounters with a few dead children in his forest route. Eadburga initially expected her husband to react in this fashion. Fortunately for her, she knew exactly what to say next. Still calm and shameless, she mentioned that all four of them will be put in danger of dying from starvation, and then chided him for thinking foolishly. Why all four may die when only two would in this case, she stressed. Then, almost insultingly, she warned him that his last woodcutting task on Earth would be preparing the planks for all of their caskets. Gundovald knew that his wife had a point, but nevertheless he would never let go of his love and care for Hansel and Gretel. As the night progressed, Eadburga continued to push her husband into abandoning his children, but still despite the family's perilous state, Gundovald continued to express his relent for his children, all while trying to keep the peace between himself and the woman that he loved.

Hunger-stricken and now suffering sleep deprivation, both Hansel and Gretel overheard their father's and stepmother's argument, while eavesdropping through their own bedroom door. What they have feared for a long while apparently was about to come true. Gretel started weeping, and mentioned to her brother that it was now their turn to be abandoned and die soon. Gretel then stressed that their stepmother would forcibly make her sinister move against them, while effectively distracting their father. Hansel, while trying to be a protective man though a very young one indeed, reassured that he would do something to alleviate this. Eventually, Gundovald and Eadburga exhausted themselves to sleep, though both knew the argument would continue, the following morning. Thankfully, Hansel did formulate a bright idea, and waited for some time after he could hear nothing from the other room but snoring. He then whispered to his sister that he must go outside to get his necessary items of his plan, while Gretel accepted any viable plan that could help them. Hansel quietly put on his coat, asked his sister to wait a moment please, and then snuck outside. He needed to find something that he would need to help them find their way home again, once they were abandoned. With the full moon, which was something he had not seen a very long time, it was not difficult for Hansel to find a lot of pebbles, near his house. The pebbles were like silver pfennigs to Hansel as he eagerly picked them all up and filled his coat pocket. When he crept back inside without making a sound, he explained to his twin sister that God would not forsake them tomorrow for Hansel had what he needed. He then confidently assured that the two could sleep in peace. Gretel was impressed with her twin brother's relaxed confidence, but she wondered what Hansel had in mind. Hansel did not yet tell Gretel his plan for he wanted to make it so secretive that there would be no chance that anything would accidentally be let out tomorrow. Gretel obliged for the time being, and both Hansel and Gretel then enjoyed their slumber.

7

The dawn broke, the next day, and it was one of the scarce clear days. However, before sunrise, Eadburga awoke her two stepchildren, and ordered them to follow their father and her into the forest to fetch some wood because their father would need some extra strength to get his work done. She then gave them each a little piece of stale bread, which she described as their dinner, following the work. She then ordered Hansel and Gretel to not eat the bread until dinnertime for they would receive nothing else to eat for the day. Hansel asked his sister to hold both pieces of bread in her dress pocket, since he had no room left in that of his coat. It was filled with pebbles. Then, the family of four set forth into the forest, with Gundovald feeling happier that he had some helping hands, and that he could continue to have wood to have for his work and their income. It was funny that Gundovald had not thought of this plan to have the whole family help him before, and it was so nice of Eadburga to offer this kind of help. Before their house began to fall out of sight as they entered the forest, Hansel stood back, glaring, while dropping a pebble onto the ground. He would repeat the process several times, until his father caught him in the act. Gundovald only asked his son what he was doing, and did not care to take notice of the dropped pebble. Hansel, having to lie, replied that he was checking back for the family cat, while wondering if it would follow them. Gundovald could not help but feel a bit touched to see his son care for any of those who lived with the family, even the cat; but Eadburga, who overheard Hansel, had a different response. Calling her stepson a fool in a non-insulting manner, she expressed that the cat would only stay home and wait for them. Then, she ordered Hansel to keep moving. His father in a nicer fashion also asked him to proceed to their forest destination. Hansel obliged without hesitation, but also worked hard to keep himself from smirking as he continued to make his trail of pebbles, just by dropping them one-by-one, while walking now.

By late morning, the family reached one of Gundovald's frequently visited areas of the forest, and then Gundovald merely asked his two children to help gather some loose brushwood and make a pile at a slightly open area in the forest. He then mentioned that he would light a fire for them, so that the children would not be cold, while they would take an occasional break from collecting workable timber. So Hansel and Gretel gathered a lot of brushwood, and made a pile from it, nearly as high as the twins' own height. Gundovald lit it, and it went aflame; and the bonfire was well controlled. After a couple of hours of helping their father collect some good timber for him to chop, Eadburga then immediately then requested that the stepchildren simply lie down and rest, while she and their father would continue cutting down, chop and gather more workable wood. Then, in a calm and reassuring manner, she stated that they would come back for them when the work was done. Hansel and Gretel at first thought that they would continue help their father and stepmother after only a short break, but Eadburga immediately protested and mentioned that the two could use some good rest, considering the long walk. Gundovald also questioned his wife about this, but with her charm, she coaxed him into her plan as well. Eadburga, who also brought a spare axe of Gundovald's, walked into the forest depths with her husband. She rubbed his back, as Gundovald brought his axe and drew the wagon onward. Hansel and Gretel looked at each other, filled with doubts, as their father and stepmother disappeared. They thought about secretly following them, but then both agreed to wait and enjoy some respite, considering that their father was there as well. Hansel and Gretel could use some rest too.

Hansel and Gretel simply sat by the fire. It kept them nice and warm, considering the cold Harz Mountain breezes. The twins kept each other good company too as always. However, hours went by and neither their father nor stepmother returned. Hansel and Gretel later figured what their stepmother had in mind for them. Indeed, it apparently was their turn to be abandoned, but Hansel had his plan, and Gretel knew that her brother had one. Gretel of course could not help but wonder what it was, but again, Hansel reaffirmed that no one should know the plan until it was ready to be implemented. Despite the situation, Hansel worked hard to hide his excitement. He could not wait to see the look on their stepmother's face, he thought. By late-afternoon, the twins ate their pieces of bread, which satisfied some of their hunger, and now they continued to wait. Their wait was not necessarily for their father and stepmother to return, but for their chance to go home themselves. For a quick moment, Hansel and Gretel actually thought that their father was near, looking for them, when they heard some wood knocking. As they looked at each other, they really did start to believe that their loving father finally learned of their stepmother's plan and now came back for them. So, the fraternal twins set out to follow the sound, while keeping the bonfire in sight. When they found the source of the knocking wood, they saw that it was only a long branch that hung from a dead tree. The wind blew the branch, allowing it to swing back and forth, occasionally knocking the tree trunk. The twin siblings grunted, wishing that their father would finally know everything. Hansel wondered why their father did not cut down and then work with this particular dead tree. It would have been perfect. Gretel nonchalantly gave her brother the obvious answer. Somehow their stepmother got the better of his judgment again and led him far from them. Back at the bonfire, Hansel and Gretel talked about many things that they used to do for fun, while their actual mother was still alive. They then comforted each other as the emotion of missing their mother started to overwhelm all other feelings. They then reassured each other that they will always have each other and their father, if they only could somehow reveal their stepmother's hatred to them in a way that their father could not contest. More hours went by as Hansel and Gretel became overcome with eventual boredom, hunger and fatigue. Both agreed to take a nap, and they fell asleep quickly.

8

Gretel awoke first and noticed that it was already night, and quickly awoke her brother. After feeling startled, Hansel quickly rose to his feet. Sure enough, they were abandoned in the forest. They noticed that the bonfire was dying but still aflame enough to maintain the warmth, but Gretel, who was feeling afraid now, angrily demanded that Hansel reveal his plan to get home. Hansel, who now knew that he could reveal it, explained that he had made a trail of pebbles all along the way from their home to their current location. He then mentioned that the waning gibbous moon must rise, so that they would have some light to enable them to easily spot the pebbles. Then, they could follow their trail home, and thankfully, it was another clear night. So, it could happen. Gretel locked her brother in a warm embrace, but then asked that if anything like this should happen again, she would be let known of a plan that Hansel may conjure up in the future as well. Hansel agreed and asked the same from his sister, should she formulate a plan like this first. Gretel thought about it and then replied maybe, but then giggled, while Hansel laughed along. With the Moon now up above, and the bonfire nearly dead, Hansel and Gretel finally set off for home. They each carried a makeshift torch, made from a simple branch to help shine their way and to deter any potential predators. Wolves and wild pigs would be a potential threat to unarmed forest wanderers, but to add to the twins' ease, no predators were near at all. The pebbles shone like silver pfennigs to Gretel as well, as both excitedly searched for the next pebble along the trail. Both even started playing a game of who would find the next pebble first, while keeping score.

By the break of dawn, the next day, the twins found their way to the edge of the forest; and from the short distance away, there it was—their home! Hansel and Gretel expressed their happiness and hugged each other again. They then started running to the front door. The two hens started clucking as if expecting to be fed, as the twins knocked. Eadburga told her husband, who was working very hard to keep fighting back his tears, that she would answer the door. Eadburga slightly flinched as she saw her stepchildren, while covering up her anger, bewilderment and frustration. The cat came to them purring, while Hansel and Gretel knelt down to pet it, while asking it if it missed them. Trying to maintain her false innocence, she called them naughty children for sleeping in the forest all night, acting as if she and their father had lost them unwillingly. Hansel and Gretel easily could not help but ignore their stepmother, while running past her and hysterically towards their father, who was exchanging his happiness and relief with them. He hugged them in a long embrace, shedding some tears of joy, since he feared that they could have been lost forever. Hansel and Gretel thought they had lost him forever as well. Eadburga stood aside watching, still concealing her anger, bewilderment and frustration. She had formulated this plan for a while, and it utterly failed. She managed to lead her husband far away from his children yesterday so that they would lose them, and yet still they survived and returned. Eadburga diligently learned and memorized a certain path in the forest that proceeded in a wide arc, which led get back home. Eadburga gave her stepchildren the false impression that she shut herself in her room to take her naps while forcibly ordering them to stay inside during many afternoons. Eadburga then snuck out to work on her child-abandonment plan in the forest, and she made trails for herself along the way, all while ensuring that she had not surprisingly bumped into her husband at work there. Carrying just enough food and a whole lot of determination in the forests, she worked hard on her plan, which she thought that she had implemented well. She led her husband in her specifically memorized path through the forest en route home, ensuring that they would avoid Hansel and Gretel and the bonfire. Yet for some odd reason beyond her comprehension, they were able to return as well. How?

It did not take long for the joyous family reunion to wane, and the family shifted back to dealing with their immense lack of food, and feeling the effects of it. An egg and a few collected wild berries were all the family could have to eat, these days. At least the family cat had recently caught a few insects and a mouse for itself. Gundovald used his one earned pfennig to purchase another slice of stale bread from town, and divided it among the four. Eadburga continued to express her authentic love for him and offered a hefty compliment for doing all the hard work possible, even if only yielding a minimal monetary return. Gundovald's hunger was often suppressed by Eadburga's expressive love, which often helped him forget about his pangs. Eadburga knew this as well, and that was why she knew she could attempt to rid her stepchildren from the household quickly again. By the evening, she then offered the heavy suggestion that the twin brother and sister must go to help their father and her in the forest again to help them collect more wood and wild berries and hazelnuts as soon as possible, or else all in the Holzhacker household will perish from starvation for certain. Gundovald did not think that Eadburga had a new abandonment plan all along, yet he was hesitant to even expose Hansel and Gretel to anything like what they had to undergo already. However, Gundovald, torn between his children and his wife, had no time to sit down and decipher her immense desire to rid his children, though she had not directly brought this up to him again. He did figure that having the whole family with him in the forest would at least let him know of everyone's momentary condition. Starting to consider it, but far from obliging, Gundovald suggested that Eadburga should occasionally share some of her food with Hansel and Gretel to show them that she really cared about them, especially what happened when they almost lost the children. Eadburga only reacted defensively at her husband, and almost in a yelling fashion, complained that he continued to put both him and her at risk for starvation. Gundovald did not know what to do, but he still did not want to bring Hansel and Gretel deep into the forest again.

That night, Eadburga thought about directly bringing up the idea of abandoning his children in the forest to her husband again in order to ensure that the two of them could finally be alone, but she knew that the result of the suggestion would be to no avail. Gundovald was indeed so grief-stricken when he thought that he may have had lost them entirely before. Gundovald actually took the first move, this time, and expressed an idea of his own, which astonished his wife and left her in a slight shock. He merely mentioned that he would rather die of starvation himself than put his two children that he dearly loved at risk for it. He then said that if he could see the three of them living even after he was gone and watching from high above, nothing would matter more to him. Eadburga could only wish her husband a good night, and lay to sleep with him thereafter. She was a bit impressed by her husband's determination for the well-being of Hansel and Gretel, but that only meant that she would have to be even more determined for the disposal of them.

Hansel and Gretel, again eavesdropped and needless to say, they knew that they had the best loving father they could ever have, when they heard him announce his willingness to give his life for them if necessary. However, they feared that their stepmother would again try to rid them again. Both calmed each other down, however, since they knew that they needed their slumber. Furthermore, the next days were Saturday and Sunday, and it was to be the times for their father to head to the marketplace and for a day of rest, and not head to the forest. So when they all woke up, the next morning, Hansel and Gretel insisted that they come with their father to help him haul the chopped wood to the marketplace, which he accepted. Eadburga declined to go for this would give her more time to secretively finish formulating her next child-abandoning plan. However for Hansel and Gretel, what a relief it was for the two to be with their father and away from their stepmother. The day was a rare sunny day with not a cloud in the sky, but with all the ground moisture, a thick mist blanketed the landscape. As Gundovald readied the wagon and the chopped wood, the twins playfully imagined themselves walking through a cloud. When it was time to proceed, Gretel helped Gundovald haul the wagon, while Hansel pushed the wagon from behind. The city gates were open with only one attending guard, not surprisingly. Gundovald and the guard exchanged waves, and the Holzhackers did their routine Saturday entry. Down the streets, they saw the mayor of Osterwieck on his carriage, accompanied by a fewer than usual number of guards. The mayor was rich and was little affected by the famine, but he surely could employ only few guards and other city workers now. As they entered the denser areas of the town, both siblings took little notice of the few remaining people in both the marketplace and the church in Osterwieck. Hansel and Gretel surely had other things to occupy their minds, despite the noticeable population drop. They and their father took the time to kneel and pray in the church for their and for all the remaining people's survival. As they progressed towards the marketplace, Hansel and Gretel took some notice of the few remaining and now-overworked horses, trudging along the town's streets with the wagons because the city streets were certainly quieter without all the cacophony of numerous clopping hooves. Gretel approached and caringly pet one of the pausing stallions, pulling a wagon. Speaking out loud, she wished for the horse's survival as well. Though the wagon driver urged the horse to keep on their way, it was not before the horse looked back at Gretel, giving her a look as if he really did understand her intentions. At last the three Holzhackers reached the marketplace, and while Gundovald set up his station with Gretel helping, Hansel took the time to examine the marketplace grounds. Hansel once found a silver pfennig here, and it would certainly be nice to find another. His luck came to him as he spotted one from a distance, but before he could react, a frail, wretched and starving adult man dove for it and grasped the coin. The adult man cradled the pfennig while heavily breathing with an ear-to-ear smile, and then ran off with the coin. Hansel knew that immense happiness could drive away hunger and fatigue, even if for only a short while, but he was a bit angry that he could not pick the coin up first, needless to say. Hansel rejoined his father and sister, and the fraternal twins were so happy to have this one chance to seclude themselves with their father. Now that the chopped wood was set up for sale, the twins expressed their own authentic fear that their stepmother had been actively trying to get rid of them, even if this meant their deaths. That was followed by the Hansel and Gretel reporting all the abuse that they continue to receive from Eadburga in his absence in full detail. Gundovald, holding Hansel and Gretel, said to his children that he preferred to maintain the peace in the household, while affirming that he loved their stepmother as well as them. Frustratingly to Hansel and Gretel, Gundovald still did not take the notion of his wife actually abusing and threatening them, and he was still fully unaware of all of this. Yet, he did reassure them that they would not be abandoned, and that he would start to monitor his wife's nature towards them in

38

secrecy to give his children some peace of mind. He then affirmed that with his monitoring, he would attempt to see if his wife was actually abusing them, and put a stop to it, even though he did not believe that all this abuse was actually happening. This brought some relief to Hansel and Gretel and the twins enjoyed their day off from their stepmother; but they later knew that they would still have new reasons to be afraid, for when evening came upon them and the three came back home, there was something to increase rather than decrease their fear. It was the fact that their stepmother was suddenly and unexplainably nicer to them throughout the rest of the weekend.

It was now Sunday evening, and on the next day, it would be time for Gundovald Holzhacker to head back into the forests to chop and collect some more wood for his own livelihood and for the family's income. Eadburga once again requested her husband to again take the children with both of them into the forest tomorrow, despite his major concerns and his initial wishes to let them stay home. Gundovald only suggested that she should stay home with them as it was before this long famine period began, despite Gundovald's limited strength and stamina. Craftily, Eadburga finally was again fully able to coax her husband into bringing the whole family after a short while with her charm. She explained that it would still be better to have two adults to gather and haul the chopped wood home, considering her husband's limited abilities. If this reason was not enough, she expressed her concern that Gundovald's strength could fully fail him and he could collapse in the depths of the forest with no one around to help him. Then, she expressed her "concern" that Hansel and Gretel may or may not remain well in their absence, and that it would be plain better to keep the children within sight. Though Gundovald felt that he had to agree again, considering these reasons, he would be careful this time for his children's sake. On the night before the family would set off into the woods again, both Hansel and Gretel were preparing to ready themselves again for the next highly likely abandonment, courtesy of their stepmother. This time, both wanted to go out and collect some pebbles in the middle of the night. They figured that they would need more pebbles to make a longer trail in the possibility that Eadburga would successfully draw them farther away from home. Though Eadburga still did not know how her two stepchildren made it back home themselves on her first attempt to abandon them, she figured out that they must have used something to help them that were beyond her knowledge and notice. So this time, she locked their bedroom door, which made Hansel and Gretel rise up quickly in startle from their beds. Trapped inside, Hansel and Gretel found that they could not sneak outside and they would have nothing to make a trail. Both of them started panicking to each other, but then they realized that since God had helped them before, God would help them again. They did not know how, but certainly there must be a way. Also, they knew that their father would keep close watch over them too.

9

The next morning, Eadburga came into the room and took Hansel and Gretel out of their beds and ordered them to get ready for the next trip into the forest. Again, she gave them a little piece of bread to each, but this time, the pieces were smaller than before. When the twins had some time alone before the family set off, they quickly started to formulate a plan to return home. Both agreed that since they could not collect anything to make a trail, they would have no choice but to use their given bread to make a trail. Hansel would use his piece of bread to make the trail by breaking off tiny but seeable morsels, while Gretel would use her piece to sustain both of them for the dayspan. Surely it was less food to sustain them overall, but they had no choice. It was surprisingly another sunny day, and for once in a long while, the grounds were not wet. Hansel and Gretel quickly recalled the times when they happily played outside before the ongoing rain and famine struck. The family of four bid farewell to the cat, and set off. Eadburga strictly mentioned to Hansel that the cat was fine before he did anything. Hansel thanked her for the notice, so that tensions would ease for now. As the four entered the forest, Hansel kept behind the rest as much as possible, reaching his hand into his coat pocket, tearing a little morsel off of the piece of bread and making a trail. He had to time himself as well as possible because both Gundovald and Eadburga checked back for him occasionally. Gundovald asked his son why he was walking behind them, thinking that he might run off somewhere. Hansel again had to make up a reason, and said that he wanted to walk a little slower to see if he could find a wild pigeon that he befriended recently. Gretel slightly snickered for she thought that that was a wonderful new excuse. Gundovald smiled back at Hansel as well and ruffled his hair, as the woodcutter father cherished anything that gave his children any hope and joy. Eadburga, however, scrunched her eyelids and shook her head in disgust and then gave Hansel a slight taunt but not one too harsh as to upset her husband. She then ordered Hansel to walk closely with the rest. Hansel and Gretel held their father's hands on each side, peeking at each other, as both knew what went on in each other's mind. Hansel used every moment that he could scrounge to use his available hand to break and let off another morsel of bread. Surprisingly and suddenly, however, Hansel found it noticeably easier to make his trail without notice because it seemed that both his father and his stepmother became immersed in a long conversation with humor. Even Hansel and Gretel found some of the statements funny, despite not being able to understand all of the adult language. Gretel gave her brother a quick smile to let him know that she felt better now, and Hansel returned a smile to let her know the same. Gretel could also see that her twin brother was fulfilling his task.

It was noontime, and Eadburga's plan was already falling in place for the family was still walking in the forest. She intended to take everyone farther away from home on this new plan that she also formulated, this time. Though she originally meant to memorize a new path home after disposing her unwanted stepchildren, Eadburga realized that a farther distance would make it harder for her to memorize a pathway back. Thus, she formulated another mode of action, ready for implementation quickly. She would just plainly lead the family farther away from home and with her craziness abandon Hansel and Gretel while she would somehow sedate her husband, while bringing him home on the same path that they had taken to get to their initial destination in the forest. Eadburga continued to stop at nothing in order to rid herself of her stepchildren and claim their father all for herself. As the four continued to progress through the trees, Gundovald did not notice that they had walked past a few Harz Mountains during his and Eadburga's long and often humorous conversations. He only stopped when he noticed that the Sun was too high in the sky. Eadburga let out some laughter to let him know that she was untruthfully not aware of the day's progression or their seemingly inexplicably long journey either. She then agreed to stop where they were, and set up their task for the day. Again, she ordered Hansel and Gretel to build a brush mound where a bonfire would be lit there. The twin brother and sister figured that they all were much farther within the Harz Mountain forests than before, but both only needed to remain close to their father. After a couple of hours of helping the adults gather some wood for them to chop, Eadburga ordered them to stay and rest at the bonfire, while the adults would set off to find and chop some more wood with her husband and without the children—no differently than last time. She again mentioned that she and her husband would come back for them when their work was done, but Hansel and Gretel most certainly knew otherwise. They were going to head to their father and keep close to him, but they noticed that their stepmother continued to successfully distract him from his children, while being affectionate towards him as they both went off. Eadburga was able to peek back at the fraternal twins with a fearfully scornful look as if virtually telling them that they better stay there where they currently were or else. Hansel and Gretel let out a yell of refusal and called for their father. Eadburga gave them the scariest sinister look that they had ever seen, while Gundovald ran to them. Hansel and Gretel begged that they stay close to their father, but Eadburga turned on her false caring mood, and said to Gundovald that the children needed a little break. Gundovald did not want to let his children out of his sight, this time, but unknowingly, his wife's persuasive charm again got the better of him at least to an extent. Hansel and Gretel had their trail of breadcrumbs, ready for them, but both preferably wanted to expose their wicked stepmother and stay near their father more than anything. Gundovald nicely asked the two to remain at the fire for just a short while, while he and his wife worked a little more. Reluctantly, Hansel and Gretel obliged. While sitting at the bonfire, Hansel and Gretel began whispering a newly formulated idea. After resting for only a few minutes, Hansel and Gretel would secretively follow their father and stepmother, and then reveal themselves when their father realized that he had been purposely led far away from them. Then, Hansel and Gretel started laughing as they started fantasizing about how Eadburga would be caught dumbfounded in the act, right in front of their father. Now, they would have their much needed proof that their stepmother was always nasty and hateful to them. Yet, both looked at each other and realized that their father would not even allow this being led away to happen from the start. However, before they knew it, again Eadburga and Gundovald disappeared from sight. Gretel screamed for her father, while Hansel lit a deadwood branch and waved it before joining his sister in their calling out. What happened? Their father promised them that he would not let them out of his sight. This could not be! Both again started yelling and screaming and waving Hansel's makeshift signal flare. Gretel lit up a signal flare as well and waved it in all directions. However, both twins grew tired quickly, after losing their energy fast from the lack of proper nourishment. Tired and suffering hunger pangs, Hansel and Gretel shared the remaining piece of bread that Gretel carried. Both twins did not feel like talking about anything now, and agreed to just lie down and rest while the bonfire flamed onward. Yet, despite their exhausted states, both knew that they would make it back home with their spare plan, and this time, their father should plainly see what their stepmother was doing to them, even if he apparently would not figure it out earlier. This gave them something to hope, but still they could not help but wonder how and why their father would remain oblivious to their abandonment a second time. Hansel promised that he would angrily question his father for doing so, the minute that they see him back home again, while imagining his stepmother being captured and put in a dungeon. Gretel wanted to push Eadburga into the muddy patch that was once their pig sty, and cite how dirty their stepmother was, both on the inside and the outside. However, now they could only rest until their eyelids weighed themselves down.

10

The bonfire was dying but again lit well enough for Hansel and Gretel as they woke up at night, which was also clear as the stars were out above them. An initial thought that came to Hansel was the notion of why such longer relief from the rainy days like this had not come before. Perhaps the long, wet spell was finally ending. Gretel immediately called out for their father again, but Hansel requested that they both remain as quiet as possible, so that they may not attract a possibly nearby wolf. Furthermore, there was no answer to her call. Gretel could not hide her frustration that they have been abandoned again, and could not help but angrily wonder again how their father could let this happen. Hansel was just as clueless, and could not help but feel angry and frustrated himself again. Then, Hansel started to rage against his stepmother, wishing full revenge against her like a knight about to fight a menacing dragon, and then Gretel had to calm things down. Now, they could only wait for the Moon to rise high enough to provide the light that the children needed. They had to wait longer for the waning gibbous phase for the visible Moon was lessening due to its orbit around the Earth. When the moonlight that they needed finally arrived, Hansel and Gretel, exhausted as they were, started looking for the nearest bread morsel. After fifteen minutes of searching the immediate path, where they came from, they found nothing. Then, they realized something that added a lot of brand new fear to their supply of suffering. There was no trail of bread morsels anymore. The birds must have had eaten all of them. Both held each other in utter helplessness. Gretel started crying, while Hansel held her tightly to comfort her, while trying to conceal his own fear of a possible wolf, springing out from the shadows at them. Even without a trail, Hansel said to Gretel that they would find the way home somehow. Gretel had her doubts, but trying was better than admitting defeat and dying in the forest. So, they each took a branch, and lit up the ends from the dying bonfire, to make torches like last time; and they set off on a path where both agreed was their best guess. Either getting back home or somehow finding their way out of the forest and reaching any village or town in Germany would satisfy them. As they walked along, both siblings held hands to make sure that if anything should happen, they would keep themselves together. When the fire from their makeshift torches almost reached their hands, they simply picked up and lit another fallen branch to make a new torch, and then stepped on the old torch until it extinguished and until the smoke fully dissipated. Even though they were tired of these thoughts, both Hansel and Gretel still could not hide their frustration that their father would allow this abandonment to happen again. Hansel and Gretel only talked in whisper as to reduce the chances of being heard by predators in the distance. As the Moon traveled along the sky, their hunger pangs eventually overcame them, and both soon decided to build and light up a new bonfire, and sleep for the rest of the night. Both were still happy that they had each other, and both were happy and relieved that they made it through the night when they woke up by early-morning, the next day.

There was going to be another clear day as the dark blue sky became lighter. Their welcome relief, however, turned to ongoing suffering as their hunger was even harsher than ever to them. Hansel and Gretel did all to keep their respective twin's spirits up when necessary, as they scrounged for anything to eat. They found only four wild berries total, but anything would do, of course. As they walked, Hansel imagined being a knight with his toy wooden sword and shield, chasing their stepmother away from the farmstead. Gretel imagined one of her flat tin dolls, talking into her ear, giving her approval to push their stepmother into the muddy patch and making sure that their stepmother would stay there and always live there. The morning had clouded up, and it started raining—the first time in a rather long while. However, the rain was welcome to the fraternal twins. Hansel and Gretel cupped their hands and drank a lot of water, while the rain continued. At least their thirst was well quenched. The rain would only last a few hours, and then the Sun came out again. Indeed both commented that the rainy days were not as common as it had been for a long time. As they continued to walk through the seemingly endless trees, Hansel and Gretel eventually grew wearier than ever as no hazelnuts or berries were to be found, and both could not walk any further. Both noticed that their ribcages were becoming visible, and began fearing death from starvation. They finally found one wild berry along the way, which they both split in two nearly equal halves. Hansel offered the slightly larger half to his sister, who knew that he cared about her a lot. She hugged him in return, but insisted on tearing off a very small bit from her half to make it even in size, which she did. With some luck on their side, they both found two more berries as the evening came about. Any berry always brightened their moods, especially in the aggravating monotony of seeing nothing but endless trees as well. They later decided to use their remaining energy to set up camp again beneath a tree, since they got to the point where they were ready to collapse. With their torches that they carried and kept lit, even in the daytime, they built up and lit another bonfire. Both held hands, and sent a prayer to God that he would help them survive this unfortunate ordeal. Then, they both went to sleep again.

Now it was two days since Hansel and Gretel had left their father's household, when the two siblings woke up, the next morning with the Sun low in the sky and with the morning mist still filling the air, which was also fresh and crisp. After quickly checking on each other that they were still here and after a brief thankfulness to God for their survival through the night again, their hunger pangs became increasingly painful. The twins licked as much dew as they could get from the leaves to get some more water albeit only a little of it this time, and set off again with lit torches. The trees were still endless as both could not bear see another tree before them. Hansel joked about the fact that they eventually should stumble upon the North Sea sometime if they were heading northward. Gretel laughed and mentioned that stumbling upon even a narrow river would suffice because then they could actually head somewhere else, following the banks. Wishing that they could somehow leave the Harz Mountain forests, both almost thought of setting some of the trees on fire, which could send a signal to let anyone, just anyone from a far distance, know that they were there and lost; but then they rescinded their idea. They did not want to start a forest fire for all the reasons, including for their own safety. They saw a red squirrel enjoying a hazelnut, which made Hansel and Gretel jealous of that sciuromorphic rodent. Yet, with their increasing weakness, even if they were to find a nut, just how would they be able to crack it open? After only a few hours of walking, Hansel and Gretel collapsed again. Holding up off the ground and clenching their torches with a weakening fist, the twins almost could only crawl on the forest floor now. They now felt that starvation was starting to approach them, which made them crawl a little faster in the hopes that they would find a single wild berry at least.

11

By midday, Hansel and Gretel saw what appeared to be a bright and beautiful, snow-white dove, which perched itself in a tree before them. It was a Eurasian collared dove, which is actually light-beige in color with a black collar around its nape, and not completely white, but to Hansel and Gretel it clearly looked as such. Both Hansel and Gretel had a reason to smile for the first time in a long while, as the dove sang melodiously. The twins happily rocked their heads in accordance to the birdsong. When it finished singing, the dove flew away and forward in the twins' own forward direction. For reasons unknown to them, their immense hunger pangs suddenly disappeared. The twins became increasingly happy, and happy to the point that they did not seem to need their torches anymore. So, they both fully extinguished them, and excitedly decided to follow the dove. Seemingly without any fatigue that they had been experiencing, Hansel and Gretel went after the bird, running, laughing and dancing along the way. It was like they were playing an enjoyable game, and all the twins could think about was the fun that came with it. Eventually, they saw their snow-white dove alighted atop the roof of a little house at a short distance from the children. The house was very pleasing in appearance and was brightly colored as well. Both siblings somehow had this urge to slumber again despite their previous burst of energy, and so they decided to check out the house out after their nap, which they both agreed towards immediately. Both Hansel and Gretel collapsed on the ground while smiling at each other. When they woke up again, it was late afternoon for they were only asleep for a few hours, this time. The dove was gone, but this beautiful, brightly colored house still stood before them. Hansel and Gretel looked at each other with ear-to-ear smiles, and leapt to their feet, and started for the house. Both siblings were playfully racing each other along the way. When they reached it, the house began to look even more pleasing, which made the twins happier than ever. Wow, it was a candy house! The walls and roof were made of gingerbread, and the roof was covered in cakes. The windows were made of clear sugar panes, and the house was decorated with confectionary. Both Hansel and Gretel stared and stared as they could not believe how all of a sudden, a house made from delightful treats, often affordable and available to only the German royalty and the aristocracy, came upon them. It was like as if someone put the house there, just for them, since the house was seemingly in the middle of nowhere within the vast forests of the Harz Mountains. Now, all they wanted to do was eat some of that house. Gretel would start on the cakes and Hansel would start on the gingerbread. Both of their mouths watered, anticipating the sweetness that they were about to enjoy. They took a full bite. Bleah! Suddenly, neither sibling felt happy anymore as their eyes started becoming hazy, and then the candy house seemed to morph into an old shack before them. The shack's gingerbread walls and roof became grey and dull wood, the cakes became fallen dead branches and twigs that mostly covered the roof, and the sugar window panes became iron bars that lined the windows. The

53

confectionary became pebbles that lay around the old shack. Both Hansel and Gretel's hunger pangs suddenly returned in full vengeance as if they never left them in the first place, which made them drop to the ground and roll over in pain and weakness. Their bodies were starving for the essential nutrients as their basic bodily functions became increasingly difficult to keep proper, and their blood sugar levels dropped significantly to the point where the amount of oxygen in their blood and brain decreased. Hence, all this time, Hansel and Gretel were hallucinating. When they struggled to their feet, both Hansel and Gretel realized that they were trying to eat nothing but deadwood. However, at this time, they surely wished that deadwood was edible, right now. Now, they both knew that the starvation process was here, and they feared their approaching death. They did not know what to do, except perhaps to lie down and die. Hansel and Gretel only wished their father could somehow come back for them and find them, as they both looked at each other sadly in the face, while lying down again in front of the shack.

A shrilly, raspy, elderly lady's voice called out from the house, asking who was there. Hansel and Gretel used their little remaining strength to raise themselves up again in curiosity, but their instincts told them that they should be afraid. They replied that they were sorry, and would be on their way; but then, the door opened. The elderly lady had long, raggedy hair and very wrinkly skin; and she stepped through the doorway. Her initial appearance was as mysteriously alarming as her voice. Afraid, Hansel and Gretel were going to try to make a run for it, despite knowing that they would shortly collapse again, not far from the house, and then maybe even die afterwards. Yet, the elderly lady only nodded her head in respect for them and gave them a shriveled but authentic smile; and in a caring manner asked the children where they came from. Hansel and Gretel remained silent and still, now not knowing what was the best reaction to take. The elderly lady, still speaking in a caring manner, invited the children inside her house, where they could have some food, since she saw that the children clearly had emaciated appearances from a long hunger span. Hansel and Gretel could not help but take a peek past her inside, and saw something delightful. There were apples, nuts and milk on her table in the main room of the house. The elderly lady knew what caught their eyes, and so she repeated her invite, while approaching them and gently holding Hansel's hand. This time, Hansel obliged and with all his remaining strength entered, and Gretel painstakingly followed them inside after the lady signaled her to do so as well. Hansel and Gretel sat on the table, and started eating the apples and nuts and drinking the milk. It was most certainly wonderful nourishment that their bodies and minds had been long awaiting. Their hunger pangs were at last quelled as the twins continued to joyfully eat. They could feel their vitality, vim and vigor returning, as both smiled without end, trying not to talk with their mouths full. The elderly lady, who seated herself on another chair at the table, asked them to stay with her for a while for she needed some company. Before Hansel and Gretel could answer, she quickly then offered them small child-sized beds in a spare room in her shack, covered with clean linen. The twins looked at each other, and then asked her if they could speak in private. She let them, as long as they would not leave the house. She actually would not have to worry about them actually leaving her home for she secretly locked the front door after the children's entrance. Hansel and Gretel agreed to stay at the shack for the moment and then went to the kitchen. They both talked it over quietly, and agreed that they should stay for at least a little while, at least for one night. That way, they could again start looking for the way back to their home with full stomachs and with high energy. So, the twins came back to the elderly lady, who still presented herself as kind and caring, and they agreed to her continued invite with smiles. Despite her rugged face, her smile was well noticeable like how it was in her introduction; and she said that no harm will happen to Hansel and Gretel, as long as they would remain with her. They asked for her name, and she merely replied that her name was Methildis. She did not care to know the children's names, however. Nonetheless, they introduced themselves as Johannes and Margaretha Holzhacker, but she could just call them Hansel and Gretel for short. Methildis gave a slight nod to make their acquaintance, but soon it would not matter for her.

Hansel and Gretel lay down on their respective beds, feeling full for the first time in ages. These beds were more comfortable than what their beds allowed them back at home. Only a noble child could sleep in such a bed, the two commented to each other. With all the wonderful food and these beds, the twins almost thought that they were in Heaven. They both joked that who thought such warmth, comfort and nourishment could come from an old shack in the middle of the woods. If they ever saw their father again, they would definitely tell him about this shack, where lived a kind elderly lady who rescued them, before mentioning the horrors of being lost in the woods while starving for a rather long while. Methildis heard the children's conversation die down, and be replaced by light snoring. She quickly peeked at them through the doorway to see them fast asleep, and then she quietly headed to her kitchen, where she began readying her kitchen. It all would start when children become enticed by the good food and the comfortable beds, she thought, like for the many lost, abandoned children that she encountered before. Then, she would enjoy her feast, which would come from one of the most disheartening acts of them all—pathological cannibalism! She quietly laughed in a sinister cackle to herself as she prepared her cauldron and her oven. Then, she went to bed herself, looking forward to her own major feast.

Hansel and Gretel woke up to another sunny morning, and felt for the first time in days, well-rested. They were full of energy, this time, and both started talking happily, anticipating finding their way home and their father almost right away. They readied themselves up, expecting a hearty breakfast, and then bidding a formal farewell to their wonderful caretaker. Methildis was already up, when they approached her in the shack's main room. Hansel and Gretel's smiles turned to sudden confusion, when she seized Hansel by the arm with her shriveled hand. Despite her old age, she certainly had enough strength to overcome a young child. It would work to her advantage, as she exited the

57

shack, locking the front door again. She then dragged him to an old horse stable that had no horse to occupy it for years, behind the old shack. Hansel first questioned what was happening in a panicked state, and wondered what he did wrong as if being punished. Methildis did not bother to answer him, and just continued to lead Hansel by force. Then, Hansel tried to wrest himself free of Methildis, while shouting out to his stunned sister, who also could not comprehend this unexplainable action; but his attempts to free himself was to no avail. She underhandedly threw Hansel into the back area of the stable, with the young boy losing balance and falling. The elderly lady locked Hansel behind a grated door, as the stable doubled as a makeshift dungeon. Hansel rose himself up to his feet and rushed to the grated door, shouting out why, but again Methildis did not reply. Hansel called out for help, but he realized that he knew that he would not be heard by anyone other. The elderly lady marched back into the shack to Gretel who tried to flee through the shack's front door, which was still locked. She screamed when Methildis grabbed her arm, as the elderly lady held her fast. Methildis then yelled that she must work for the homeowner now. As Gretel's first assignment as a slave, Methildis yelled at her to fetch some water, and help her cook some stored fatty animal meat, which would later be fed to her brother. Methildis admitted that she was going to cannibalize her twin brother when she said that she would do so after fattening him up. Gretel screamed in terror and sadness, but she was only slapped by the elderly lady, and would not stop slapping her until she stopped screaming. Gretel would have no choice but to assist this evil "Old

Witch of the Forest" (whom she now referred towards) for the time being as her new slave, and she knew that she would be cannibalized next. With her red facial marks still stinging, Gretel worked hard to fight back the tears of pain.

Methildis had Gretel shackled to one of her ankles with an iron chain that was attached to a heavy iron ball on the other side. The chain was long enough, so that Gretel could move about the shack and within its immediate surroundings, but no farther. The chain was indeed long enough for Gretel to be able to reach the elderly lady's personal well, at a short distance behind her shack. The iron ball was heavy enough to slow a small child down considerably, should one attached to it tried to run away. The shackle held her tightly, and she knew that she could not do anything to free herself. She saw the stable further behind the shack, where she knew that her brother was kept hostage. However, en route to the well, carrying an empty bucket, Gretel accidentally tripped over what at first appeared to be a metal hook. Closer examination confirmed it, as Gretel became curious of it. She then noticed that the hook opened a trapdoor in the ground, and the door was covered in rocks, dirt and foliage. Had she not stumbled upon the hook, she would not have noticed the concealed trapdoor, but she did. Partially clearing this trapdoor, Gretel lifted the door open. What she saw inside made her close the trapdoor very quickly though quietly, and made her horrified and teary eyed as she crossed herself may times, breathing heavily. Then, she quickly restored the door's coverings. Very reluctantly but hurriedly, she brought back the bucket of water from the well to fill the witch's cauldron that hung over the hearth. Gretel hurried back as fast as she could, so that the "Witch" may not suspect of Gretel's discovery, and thankfully, the "Witch" did not suspect anything. Methildis then prepared a stew, with meat and vegetables, for herself and Hansel, while Gretel only received discarded crabshells, from brown crabs that lived in the North Sea, to eat. It was little food for Gretel, but still noticeably more than what she managed to find in the forest with her brother. So at least for now, she did not suffer hunger and weaken unlike before. Gretel noticed that the "Witch" had an oven, which was suspended on an iron stand that rolled on four wheels, and also meant to be placed above the hearth when in use. She noticed that the hanging cauldron could be easily moved, since it was hung on a ceiling track with a track wheel that affixed the cauldron's three chains. Gretel also noticed that the "Witch" was quite a skilled cook and the stew smelled really good. As she ate her discarded crabshells, she could not help but notice that the "Witch" clearly had enough food for herself. So, why would she need to cannibalize small children? Furthermore, where did she get all this food? If those were not enough, Gretel saw that the "Witch" definitely had enough strength to make it on her own, despite her senile appearance. It was somewhat amazing but how? Gretel's puzzlement was almost as strong as her worry for her brother, and for the fear for their lives…and for the shock of her new discovery beyond the hidden trapdoor. At night, Methildis threw Gretel into the children's bedroom, and locked the door. Needless to say, there was no wishing of a good night. With only some outdoor moonlight peering inside the room,

Gretel discovered a small chest against the far wall of the bedroom, full of expensive toys, made for richer children. There were detailed clay-based dolls for the girls and clay-based knight string-puppets for the boys. So, she brought the dolls out, and quietly began playing with them. As she was about to take full advantage of dolls' play value, she realized that other girls must have been playing with these same dolls, prior to what ultimately happened to them. She then realized that other boys must have once played with these knight string-puppets. This again reminded her of her discovery, but now this only made her want to find a way for her and her brother to escape with more determination.

12

Methildis, the "Old Witch of the Forest", brought much food to the incarcerated Hansel in the stable, by next morning. She raised a small door at the bottom of the grate that was large enough for only a plate or a bowl of food, then placed a large bowl of stew through it, and then yelled at Hansel to eat it all, while Hansel sat on the ground, angry, silent, frightened and bewildered. He knew that saying anything in response would be for naught. As the "Old Witch of the Forest" (who he also referred the elderly lady as such) marched back outside, Hansel reached for the stew, which was quite a delicacy. There was surely a lot of stew to enjoy, and the bowl was large enough to feed a few people. The stable that incarcerated him was dark and dingy, and his only major light source was from a small barred window—originally meant for a horse's fresh air—within the "dungeon". Occasionally, he could hear his captor yell out commands, throughout the day, which gave him relief and the reassurance that his sister was at least not dead or immensely tortured. Hansel hoped that either he could escape and rescue Gretel and leave immediately or vice versa. Either way, Hansel was not going to let himself just sit there at the mercy of this old "Witch". He then started comparing this old "Witch" to his stepmother, and actually could not determine who was worse to him. Either way, Hansel had to find a way out somehow, even if he would have to get his hands dirty. He smiled to himself as he formulated an idea. After finishing his meal and being fully energized, he started digging at the most dimly lit corner of the "dungeon" at the opposite wall from the window. Making a way out for himself certainly would keep his spirits up; even if escape would take a long time for there was a lot of digging to do. Furthermore, working on an actual escape plan would be a lot better than plainly sitting in total boredom while the Sun travelled across the sky and setting afterwards. A few days went by, and Methildis continued to give Hansel a large tray of food, while the young boy faked despair as he slowly started eating. When the "Witch" left the stable, Hansel manifested his overall calm state to himself, and there were reasons to be happier for there were ham, eggs, apples, milk, bread, stew, oats, pork and honey-sweetened desserts—delicious! He was given a lot of water as well. At first Hansel ate almost all the offered food, stopping only when uncomfortably full. However, it was not long until he ate only until he was satisfied, leaving extra food untouched. There was something ostensible about all of this, and there had to be some odd reason why Hansel was being non-subtly overfed. He resumed his digging when he could, expending his acquired energy.

More days went by, and Methildis continued to enslave Gretel and keep her chained. The shackle never once left Gretel's leg, since being placed there by the "Witch". Methildis also continued slapping Gretel at anytime that she disobeyed. Gretel's anger was surely mounting, and she thought that her stepmother was nasty. The "Witch" went one morning to check on Hansel's fattening process. However, Hansel to her dismay was not getting fat. He

63

remained his normal weight. Though she did not admit it to him, Hansel eventually learned that the elderly lady was going to cannibalize him. It was the only explanation for all the extra food. So, he did not eat more than he needed, though it was certainly tempting at times. Hansel did eat one of her desserts that were included in the meals every now and then, but he threw the extra food outside the stable window, where scavenging animals enjoyed their feast whether day or night. He made sure that he would not give the impression to the "Witch" that he was disposing the extra food, but nonetheless leaving her an empty plate. Hansel was full of energy, and continued to work on his secret escape route. Like his sister, Hansel also wondered about all the food that the "Witch" had, and why she would find the need to cannibalize anyone, but escape with his sister often took precedence in his mind. One morning, Hansel woke up, expecting his "breakfast", when instead the "Witch" unlocked the grated door and barged into his cell, which made him back to the wall in fear as he watched a frightening semi-silhouette advance towards him. Methildis grabbed him and as he let out a short shout, she flattened his face to the ground. Then, with a long piece of cloth, she forcefully tied his mouth shut. Then, as quickly as she entered his cell, she locked the grate again, and ran outside the stable, and shut the door. Methildis burst into the "guest room" where Gretel just woke up. She let out a short scream as she saw the "Witch" run towards her and forcefully cover her mouth and then also flatten her face to the floor. Methildis also tied her mouth shut with a long piece of cloth, and quickly closed and locked the door after leaving. Both Hansel and Gretel, though apart from each other, had the exact same kind of thoughts racing through their heads. Furthermore, from both of their respective locations, the twins could faintly hear another voice besides that of the "Witch". It was that of an adult man, though they knew that it was not their father. Hansel reached for the stable window's bars, and pulled himself up just to catch a glimpse of who else was out there. Gretel climbed onto the other bed to peep out the window in order to also catch a glimpse of who else was out there as well. It took both twins some extra effort to get just the right viewing angle that they needed to catch that intriguing view of who was there with "The Old Witch of the Forest". Both Hansel and Gretel simultaneously fell back in their respective locations in shock, even though they saw who was with the "Witch" for only a short second. He was undeniably a knight, and with an impressive surcoat, decorated in bright sky blue and gold colors, over his armor. His banner's colors matched those of his surcoat. They also quickly saw his squires bring barrels and buckets towards the shack, and they saw a few horses with them all. Though Hansel could not hear it because he was in the stable, Gretel could hear these barrels and buckets being brought into the shack's storeroom. Both then faintly heard the knight and the "Witch" finish their conversation, heard a few neighs from the horses; and then there was silence. The "Witch" reentered Hansel's and Gretel's locations and forcefully removed their mouth binds, and then all had returned to "normal". Who was this knight and why was he here? The fraternal twins surely had another question to mull. Hansel could not help but think about his toy wooden sword and shield, back home, as well, while

Gretel held one of the clay knight string puppets, trying to formulate theories on the knight's ordeal here. Hansel imagined himself as the knight going after the "Witch", which made him laugh to himself. Gretel only exited the room to obey her next order.

A few more days had gone by, and Gretel continued to work as a slave for Methildis, while Hansel continued to be held in the stable "dungeon". One morning when the "Witch" was bringing Hansel's hearty breakfast, he extended an old discarded hambone out to receive the food. He found it within the "dungeon" and tried to jokingly fool the "Witch" into thinking that he was deathly skinny for not eating much. The "Witch" only roared at the boy for wasting her time. She also yelled at Hansel for she now knew that he was intentionally not eating all the food that she was offering to him, since he was not becoming fatter. Hansel in retaliation built up the courage to refuse all the extra food in front of her, and say that he hoped that he would taste bad after she tries to eat him. Hansel's refusal to fatten himself up along with his cleverness to uncover her plot overcame Methildis's patience. So, she stormed out of the stable and grabbed the still-chained Gretel and brought her into the stable to see her brother for the first time in many days. Seeing each other brought them happiness for only a split second for Methildis already started yelling at her slave. The "Witch" loudly ordered Gretel to tell her twin brother that he must fatten himself up with all the extra food or she would face another round of slapping in her brother's presence, while the "Witch" mentioned that she would cook and eat Hansel soon anyway. Should Hansel cooperate by fattening himself up, Methildis told them that both would remain alive for a little longer at least on their behalf. Stirring up some courage, Gretel talked back to her captor for the first time, by saying that the "Witch" may not have had them from the beginning, had a wolf pack found them in the forest first. Hansel could not help but grin. As unfortunately expected, however, Methildis slapped Gretel again, but this time with higher than usual force as if swinging her arm to whack her, and then the "Witch" yelled at her to not talk back to her again. Hansel could only look onward, stunned as if feeling the same pain. Though some tears flowed from Gretel's eyes from the searing pain from her cheeks, her anger continued to rise. Hansel wanted to yell back at their captor, but did not since it may incite another round of strikes against his sister. The "Witch" quickly shoved Gretel forward, where she impacted against the grated door. Hansel and Gretel both did not say a word to each other, and just reached their hands through the grate holding each other's, while Gretel shed some tears, and even Hansel shed one and their eyes locked on each other's as well. Neither twin was embarrassed to let a tear flow down his and her cheek, as they finally saw how each other was held captive in their different respective ways. Methildis again ordered Gretel to recite the warning for Hansel, but the young girl turned around and only yelled no. Hansel could not bear to see his twin sister get slapped repetitively in front of him again. So this time, Hansel yelled at the "Witch", calling her an old whey-faced haggard. It managed to catch the attention of the "Witch" for she stopped slapping Gretel and turned her shriveled, enraged face towards the jailed brother of her temporary slave. Hansel refused to be frightened by her, and again called her an old whey-faced haggard in a threatening and insulting voice tone. Methildis threw Gretel to the ground, and removed a sharp iron prod stick that was hung from the stable wall, and then snarled; and while reaching through the grate, attempted to prod Hansel with a stabbing force. She initially missed, but the games had begun. Hansel did his best to dodge the "Witch's" prod stick, and he most certainly had to do so, or she may inflict a serious or mortal wound in him. She yelled in frustration as she missed and missed her captive, who occasionally let out a confident laugh when she missed him with the prod, but Hansel surely wished that he had a sword right now. With her evil-looking face, filled with rage, Methildis diligently continued her attempts to prod Hansel through the grate, while shouting, as he began worrying that she would not stop until she hit her target. The "Witch" loudly yelled at him to stand still, but Hansel only called her a whey-faced haggard again before blatantly refusing. Then on another attempt to stab him, the prod stick nearly missed Hansel after another successful dodge, but Hansel used the closeness of the prod to his advantage. He grabbed the other side of the prod, while half of it was still on his side of the grate, and he kept hands and his body away from the sharp point, and never in front of it, needless to say. Hansel was ready to retaliate with an enraged, determined face, as he and the "Witch" tugged with all their might for possession of the prod. Methildis snarled at Hansel with her evil shriveled face in the attempt to frighten him, but Hansel was not afraid, and gave her a growl in return as if he was posing as a caged beast waiting for the right chance to strike back upon finding freedom. Hansel also used his feet to push against the grate, which gave him some extra force against the strength of the "Witch". Methildis yelled at the top of her lungs to Hansel to let go of the prod, but Hansel outwardly said no, and once again called her a whey-faced haggard. Determined, Hansel certainly found new strength to counteract that of the "Witch". If only he had it before he was imprisoned, but thus far, the victor of this tugging match had yet to be determined. The "Witch" then heard herself loudly being called a maggot-pie by Gretel, who delivered a strong kick with her unchained leg to the back of Methildis's right knee. The "Witch" felt the jarring pain, and quickly lost balance and fell backwards, followed by her yelling out in agony. Hansel fell backwards too, inadvertently throwing the prod against the back wall. He quickly picked up the prod, and quickly handed it to his sister through the grate, so she could protect herself. Gretel quickly picked the prod up and held it, pointing forward to the astonished Methildis, who helped herself back up from a distance. The "Witch" yelled at the top of her lungs for Gretel to drop the prod, but Gretel, who was also filled with rage, held the prod fast; and she would not hesitate to use it on Methildis as if it were a cavalry lance, should the "Witch" take one step closer to her. Hansel hoped that Gretel would not loosen her guard or the rage on her face, while he worked on catching his breath. He would certainly have done the same if he were in her shoes. Gretel did not move a single muscle, and kept her eyes ever so focused on the "Witch". Methildis yelled the order again to drop the prod. Gretel kept her stance and her focus strong.

Methildis slowly retreated, keeping her eyes on Gretel and her weapon, as she backed out of the stable, and slammed the door with Gretel's chain under it. The twins then quickly heard the stable door lock up. Gretel for a moment thought that Methildis would try something else like tugging the chain from beyond the door, but after several minutes, nothing happened. Finally Hansel and Gretel could let themselves talk to each other again. Though both held each other's hands through the grate again, both siblings kept their eyes more on the door than on each other, while Gretel never let go of the prod with her other hand. Yet, both could not help but give each other a virtual embrace as their clenching of each other's hand became tighter, and they both complimented each other on their first retaliatory fight against the "Witch". They both thought that neither would see the other again, and then they both brought up their father again, still wishing that somehow, he would suddenly break open the door and rescue them. However, they feared that their father may now think that his two children had died in the forest, and were dragged off by wolves to their den perhaps. However, Hansel and Gretel for the first time in many days could not help but bring up something fun as well, despite the grated door between them and the "dungeon" walls all around them. Both slightly elevated their spirits as they started playing their favorite games, through the grate, and both heard each other laugh in such a way for the first time, since they had the company of their loving parents. They then mentioned that had their mother, Hiltrude, seen their successful fight against the "Witch", she would have been so proud of them. They also knew that their father

70

would have been proud of them too. They still, however, never let the stable door out of their sights, and Gretel kept the prod stick right next to her. When nightfall arrived, both promised that one would stay awake while the other one would sleep, and take turns. Unfortunately, of course, both young children fell fast asleep.

13

When Methildis woke up, the next morning, she decided to change her big feasting plans. Considering how Gretel had given her a lot of difficult times (without thinking that she had done much more of that to Gretel), the "Witch" out of anger decided to cannibalize Gretel first instead. She would roast Gretel in the oven, and then feast on her in the stable where her brother could see them. This would most certainly deliver the ultimate insult to Hansel, before she would kill and consume him later. Her facial wrinkles moved accordingly as she formed a confident, sinister smile, while nodding and chuckling to herself. She went outside to the stable, and she silently unlocked and opened the door, and effortlessly picked up and hung back up the prod stick. Then with the most falsifying smile, she gently woke up Gretel, while grasping her arm. Both Hansel and Gretel woke up suddenly, and both tried to react accordingly, but it was too late. Hansel and Gretel shouted out for each other, making a futile attempt to reach for each other, but the "Witch" mentioned with her smile that Gretel should not have been so naughty in raspy-voiced baby talk, while shaking her index finger at her. Methildis dragged Gretel out of the stable and back to the shack, while Gretel still angrily tried anything that she could to wrest herself free, but all to no avail. Hansel feared for his sister's life, while he quickly went back to his own escape plan. Hansel built up some confidence and humored himself by imagining Methildis and his stepmother

Eadburga fighting each other. Then, Hansel's determination filled his mind, knowing that the "Witch" was not going to get away with her evil acts. Never before has Hansel's hands been dirtier as Hansel vigorously dug. Gretel sat on the kitchen floor, and this time, she was unable to move far for the "Witch" shortened the chain. She then ordered Gretel that should she say one word, she would slap her miserably again. The "Witch" lit up the hearth, and mentioned to Gretel that she would bake a new loaf of bread for Hansel and herself. Gretel saw Methildis kneading the dough, readying it for baking, while Gretel tried to formulate an escape plan.

Methildis wheeled the oven over the hearth. Then, she pushed Gretel towards the oven, where the hearth flames were already blazing underneath. The "Witch" was almost going to ask Gretel to crawl inside the oven to check to see if the oven was warm enough inside before placing in the bread dough, and then she would shut the oven door, trapping Gretel; but then she figured that the young girl would not fall for it. So, Methildis decided to do something more direct. The "Witch" crouched down to the seated Gretel who had her arms crossed, and then Methildis decided to reveal more of herself to Gretel before the young girl became her next meal. With her shriveled face and a sinister smile, she admitted to Gretel that she was eighty-five years old (which was a surprisingly old age for anyone in medieval Europe), and that she resorted to cannibalism of the dead during the Great Famine, but she was not among the hungry. So, it was not survival-cannibalism. She rhetorically asked Gretel if the girl noticed all the food that the "Witch" already had to her needs. She said that someone special always delivered food to her, every week, so she was never hungry. However, there was one thing that she always wanted. She always wanted to restore her youth, so she thought she would practice witchcraft that could enable her to do so. Her attempts at this came about a year ago, when she stumbled upon a recently dead abandoned child, near her shack. She decided to cook and eat the child, while thinking that she would slowly but surely start ageing backwards from the consumption of juvenile flesh. To her welcome surprise, she felt a sense of newfound strength and stamina after doing so. So, she quickly acquired a taste for the flesh of small children, and then she continued to believe that cannibalizing little youths would keep her alive longer and longer, while she became younger and younger. She also believed that she would be able to retain her needed strength and then regain lost old strength from her practice. To the bewildered Gretel, Methildis's mood changed to authentic delightful enthusiasm as she said that she was looking forward to looking and feeling like a twenty-year old woman again at the age of one hundred. So, she then began the practice of capturing abandoned children in the forest and then murdering them for consumption after nourishing and fattening them up with regular food, whenever the possibility arose. This possibility came about quite often to the "Witch's" delight over the short yearspan of finding wandering abandoned children. She ate the children fresh, and all of her other food—her fruits and vegetables, her meat, her milk, her bread dough, etc. that she had would only be supplemental nourishment for her. Finally, the "Witch" again happily reiterated that she would one day be a young and beautiful woman again. She faced and cackled at Gretel, who now fully understood that she was going to "assist" Methildis on her witchcraft practice as her next meal and for the fact that Methildis was an actual witch after all. Now, Methildis was to force Gretel into the oven, by first picking up and throwing Gretel's ball and chain inside, and then shoving Gretel in afterward. The "Witch" told Gretel to not to worry for the ball and chain will eventually cool off after she would extinguish the flames, so she could use them again. Then, she wielded a dagger to ensure that Gretel's had nowhere to go but inside. Methildis, still smiling with her shriveled, sinister face, simply mentioned that it was now time to prepare Gretel as her next meal, and enjoy her in front of her brother before consuming him later. Gretel's newfound confidence to protect herself again was lost as the "Witch" brought forward the sharp dagger closer to her neck. Feeling a little sense of distress, Gretel tried one more thing to somehow help her avoid this awful death. She looked at the "Witch" with an incontestably meaningfully sad face, looking eye-to-eye with her, trying to get any mercy from her captor. Methildis only angrily said that she had seen this before many times, and it would not work. Grabbing Gretel one more time by the arm with her other arm, Methildis forcefully said to the young girl that if she would not move herself into the oven right away, the "Witch" would simply stab her to death on the spot. Pick your death, she sadistically ordered Gretel, for the end result would be the same.

In Gretel's peripheral vision, she saw someone at the front door of the shack, wielding a horse prod. Gretel immediately built up all her strength to save herself and announced to the "Witch" that it was actually her death that had come. She punched the "Witch" in the eye, which stunned her in pain, and which allowed Gretel to wrest herself free. The "Witch" applying pressure to her eye, swung the dagger, but it missed Gretel. Gretel then darted forward with all her might to move away from the reach of the "Witch's" dagger, and it was also enough to pull the ball and chain out of the oven. Immersed with this completely unexpected pain, Methildis growled and turned around with rage as she stood up and raised her dagger and pointed it downward, as she readied to stab Gretel to death. However, the "Witch" became immediately distracted and puzzled when she suddenly saw Hansel running towards her in a knightly charge with the prod, and emitting a battle cry. Hansel almost expected the "Witch" to engage in a mock swordfight with her dagger against his prod. Gretel, who still continued to pull the ball and chain, managed to pull the hot smoldering iron ball to Methildis's feet and ankles, which made contact. The searing burning pain overcame her quickly as she dropped her dagger, while howling and hopping. Gretel turned around, and with a loud, angry and forceful cry of her own, gave the "Witch" a strong push in the direction of the oven and the hearth. Methildis's body pushed the oven over to its side, while her head and shoulders fell directly onto the blazing hearth. The flames engulfed her head, upper body and clothes immediately, while the "Witch" yelled out the most agonizing screams that anyone could hear. The "Witch" tried

76

to roll herself away but it was too late, the flames already had a grip on her, and she lost all her remaining strength. Both twin siblings saw Methildis's clothes catch on fire as well, but then Hansel tugged his twin sister's arm, and both started heading to the front door. By pulling the chain that was not initially in the oven with his free hand, Hansel gave some extra strength to Gretel as she had to draw the ball and chain with her. Methildis, the evil "Old Witch of the Forest" had burnt to death. From the front door, Hansel and Gretel noticed that the fire caught onto the wooden furniture, and was spreading. They quickly ran outside, and Gretel told Hansel about the storeroom around the shack and towards the back door, where much food was stored. The first thing they saw was a bucket of apples, so they quickly brought it outside before the flames reached the storeroom. The twin siblings then ran far enough away from the shack, which was now fully on fire. They continued to watch it until the whole shack burnt down and nothing but waning smoke remained.

14

Hansel and Gretel kissed each other, and hugged each other so tightly that they lost balance and fell to the side, which did not bother them for they were still locked in embrace. They kept their arms around each other for at least ten minutes. When they both calmed down, they realized that they still had to find their way out of the forest and back home. At least they had some food to carry with them, this time. In what were the private quarters of the "Witch", Hansel and Gretel discovered a chest that was partially burned with a large hole at the top. They looked inside, and they saw a set of keys on a ring along with a vast stow of coins, jewels and pearls. After the children recovered from the welcome shock, they tried each and every key until they found the one that unlocked Gretel's shackle, which finally freed her from the ball and chain. Gretel massaged her ankle in utter happiness for it was more than great to have that shackle dislodged at last. Then they began laughing and circle-dancing, which they had not done for a long time. Then, they both filled their pockets with the money and valuables, and then both agreed that they should leave this place now. Hansel first quickly showed Gretel his completed escape route from the stable that he dug up himself under one of the stable walls. Gretel certainly admired her brother's cleverness. Then, just like how it was before they stumbled onto the house of "The Old Witch of the Forest", they set forth again. Passing through the trees, indeed it was just like before, but this time, they were not starving and they had food with them. They used the prod stick to share the weight of the bucket of apples as they went along. Both shared each other's personal stories of being held captive by the "Witch", as they continued to feel happy, proud and relieved. Gretel complimented Hansel on his cleverness, and Hansel did the same for Gretel on her bravery. When they would find their home again, they jokingly agreed that they would take their father with them and slip away from the old farmstead and their stepmother. Both twins then realized, while looking confidently at each other, that they would be prepared to deal with their stepmother, considering what they had already overcome. Then, they would use the newly acquired money to purchase a new and better home for themselves and their father. Two hours later, they stumbled upon a narrow path. Happy to have found any defined path, they were just about to follow it, when they started hearing the clopping of horses' feet. Then, a knight (accompanied by his squires), who was the same knight that both children had independently saw earlier from the now-burnt shack, approached them. The knight raised his helm visor, and asked them if the children were lost. Hansel and Gretel preferred to be left alone, considering what has happened, but both twins feared that the knight would look for the now-dead "Witch" for some odd reason if they said no, since he knew her. So, Hansel and Gretel said yes, but kept the secret from him. The knight ordered his squires to have the twins ride with them, and all were to bring the fraternal twins back to their home with them. The knight knew the way to Osterwieck, and the way there happened to be along the defined pathway.

It was late afternoon of the same day of their escape, when the knight brought Hansel and Gretel to their home. The twins always carried faith that they would one day return home, though both knew that it was quite hard to keep that faith for a while. Gundovald Holzhacker stepped out from the front door, and Hansel and Gretel dismounted and screamed for their father, running hysterically, while Gundovald stared and stared with his mouth open, not moving a muscle. Even after the impact while Hansel and Gretel lay atop their father on the ground, kissing and embracing his arm and face, Gundovald still could not believe his eyes, as he lay face-up on the ground, maintaining a fixed stare to the sky. The knight, with his visor up, approached them and jokingly asked Gundovald if they were his children, though he easily could tell. Gundovald finally had the energy to speak and replied yes. The knight only mentioned that Gundovald should be careful for his children's sake because it could be dangerous out there in the vast Harz Mountain forests. The knight knew that Gundovald's children were not lost in the forest due to possible negligence on Gundovald's behalf, but he just simply bowed to the knight in agreement. The knight confidently smiled and nodded in acknowledgment, and ordered his squires to head back into the forest with him. Gundovald continued to hold his children, still trying to comprehend that his children, Hansel and Gretel, had survived despite their absence for a few weeks, and are back home with him. He admitted that he thought they had died in the forest. The twins were about to tell a very long story of their near-death adventures when they quickly realized with some fear that they totally forgot about their wicked stepmother. Their father assured them that they would not have to worry anymore about her, while feeling partially sad. Gundovald decided to tell his story first, and Hansel and Gretel obliged because they were curious as to what happened during their absence and how their stepmother managed to leave them in the forest again.

Gundovald mentioned that on that unfortunate day when he lost sight of his children in the forest, while his wife Eadburga led him away, he insisted that they return to the children's vicinity. When she refused and tried to lead him further away, he finally confronted her on why. In a demanding fashion, he asked her if her whole plan was to abandon them, right then and there. She then flew into rages and then admitted that she never loved his children and only wanted to dispose of them. To Eadburga, Hansel and Gretel only got in the way of her life, which was her life that she wanted to spend with Gundovald only. Gundovald then forcefully announced that he would leave her, and then started back to his children. However, what he remembered next was finding himself bandaged in the head, and tied to his bed, back at his home. He could still feel the pain from a blow. He later learned that his wife hammered him with the poll of her axe, knocking him out, and then used the wagon to haul him home. Eadburga was concerned for she did not know the way home, and was simply only heading in the rough direction from where they came. However, with a stroke of luck, Eadburga stumbled onto a pathway. As she continued to draw her unconscious husband down the path, Eadburga encountered a travelling merchant who had a horse-drawn wagon. The merchant answered her fake calls of distress that her husband was attacked by a bandit in the forest, and had to be brought home in Osterwieck for medical attention immediately. When he regained consciousness, the immobilized Gundovald then saw his wife, coming in smiling and walking suggestively, saying that at last they were alone. Eadburga was going to try to seduce him as always, but for once he refused her, and then yelled that she killed his children. She then angrily slapped him, and only said that it would be only a matter of time till he would forget about Hansel and Gretel. Eadburga then heard someone at the door, and told him that she would return shortly in a falsely caring voice, while Gundovald struggled to free himself to no avail. Adalberta, his first wife Hiltrude's sister, was right there at the front door, which stunned Eadburga. After she stormed inside, she mentioned that she was only coming for a long-awaited visit, but overhead what had happened just from standing and eavesdropping from outside, and then called Eadburga a very poor excuse for a wife, and was going to turn Eadburga in to the mayor of Osterwieck. Then, a fierce wrestling match took place between Adalberta and Eadburga, while the immobilized Gundovald could only hope that his sister-in-law would win the fight. After sustaining a few blows, Adalberta managed to pin Eadburga and punch her incessantly, until she surrendered. Enraged, the aunt of Hansel and Gretel ordered Eadburga to leave her brother-in-law's home and never return. Eadburga turned to Gundovald and declared her love for him again, but Gundovald gave his wife a dirty look while also mentioning that he never wanted to see her ever again as

Eadburga left sadly and heartbroken. Adalberta saw her disappear into the forest surprisingly. The next day, Eadburga was found dead there, killed by wolves, and partially consumed. Adalberta got closer to Gundovald as she nursed him back to health, but he dearly missed his children. He also expressed his wishes that if only Eadburga could have given Hansel and Gretel a chance, they would have benefited her life as well, but she remained so one-sided. Then, Gundovald wished that he could have taken his children's complaints more seriously, when he had the chance, but he only got more angrier at himself for not doing so and sadder for his now-dead children that he loved. Adalberta understood his grief and continued to comfort Gundovald. Adalberta forgave him for she understood what troubles he was facing, and caringly mentioned that it was not his fault. Relieved, Gundovald thanked her dearly. Adalberta also mentioned that she recently left her husband, since she could no longer take his drunken abusiveness. Eventually, Adalberta and Gundovald formed a relationship and Gundovald had once again a new reason to push forward in life. Indeed having Adalberta would be a wonderful new start for his life, even though he would still be a poor woodcutter. Adalberta mentioned that their love was stronger than money, and they would be very happy together once the wedding ceremony would commence. He knew that she was right, especially after enjoying a warm kiss with her.

Hansel and Gretel were touched by the story. Then Gundovald asked his fiancé to step out from the kitchen, and Hansel and Gretel ran over to embrace their aunt, who was just as happy to see them. Then, both adults sat down, and wished to hear the children's story. Gundovald and Adalberta at times exchanged looks of shock as they could not believe what happened. During the story, Hansel also learned from his sister of the ultimate intentions of the "Witch", and he now fully understood everything as well. Gundovald and Adalberta remained appalled by what nearly happened to them, and that made them kiss and embrace the children more for Hansel and Gretel indeed almost could have easily died in this Methildis's shack in the middle of the forest. Both Gundovald and Adalberta also complimented their bravery and cleverness, and their diligence to always stick together and work together, and to keep the faith. The adults also sneered at the defeated, wicked elderly lady's pathological-cannibalistic tendencies of small children, yet continued to remain amazed at how Hansel and Gretel were able to overcome her, especially when it really mattered the most. However, Gundovald and Adalberta began to be a little concerned about the knight who brought the children home. While Hansel and Gretel brought out the money and jewels from Methildis's burnt home, Gundovald and Adalberta were pleasantly surprised, and agreed to the children's plans to have all of them leave this old farmstead and start a new, richer and more secure lifestyle. Yet, Gundovald and Adalberta started fearing the knight who seemingly had a relationship with the now-dead elderly lady now. So, Gundovald and Adalberta told Hansel and Gretel that it was time for dinner—something that the twins were so happy to enjoy with family again—and then tomorrow morning, all of them would set off, perhaps to another town, where they would then live. That night, the twins looked at their toys for the first time in a while. Hansel and Gretel never thought that their inexpensive toys would feel more valuable than the expensive toys at the "Witch's" burnt shack until now. Hansel and Gretel could not help but stay awake for a while longer in sheer excitement, and then they both knew that at last, they could sleep in utter peace and comfort—the first time, since their loving mother was last with them. They also knew that their father as well as they would enjoy the love and companionship of their Aunt Adalberta, who Hansel and Gretel would later call Mother as well. Prior to falling asleep, the family cat also paid a visit to the twins with some welcome-home purring.

15

The next morning, Gundovald and Adalberta quickly ordered Hansel and Gretel to pack their clothes and toys, as they would have to abandon their stead. Hansel and Gretel were slightly bewildered by the apparent rush, but they later shrugged their shoulders. The adults kept their two chickens with them, as the Holzhacker family with their cat would set on foot through Osterwieck and then on the road to the next town. However, as the adults feared, the same knight approached them all before they could leave, and the knight was accompanied by a greater entourage of squires. Hansel and Gretel plainly said hi first, but even they knew that this would not be a warm greeting. The knight, raised his visor to allow the family to recognize him again, and identified himself as Herr Gerhardt Hochberg, and firmly questioned Hansel and Gretel about whether or not they had any knowledge of the death of the elderly lady of the burnt shack, who was also his mother, in the forest. The knight then mentioned that it would advisable that they would not lie to him, while his squires started approaching the family too. Hansel and Gretel hid behind Gundovald and Adalberta, peeking out to the imposing knight and replied yes, then crunched their eyelids. Both Gundovald and Adalberta dropped to a knee, and quickly tried to plead with the knight that his mother was going to kill and cannibalize them, and that Hansel and Gretel had to kill her out of complete self-defense. While the adults pleaded with Herr Gerhardt

Hochberg, he noticed the two children peeking towards him, nodding in agreement with the adults with the most fearful but serious faces that he had ever seen. The knight stepped off of his horse, approached Hansel and Gretel, kneeling to them closely. He asked them to come forward and promised that he would not hurt them. When they came forward, the knight asked in a softer voice tone if there was anyway to prove any of this to him. Hansel scrambled to collect his thoughts, while Gretel stepped forward almost eye-to-eye with the knight and confidently but respectfully answered that they could indeed prove it to him. Hansel jerked his head to his sister in utter surprise. Gretel then mentioned that if they all return to Methildis's stead, she could prove it to everyone. Gundovald and Adalberta found some relief in this, of course, but what could the proof be? The knight then lowered his visor, and ordered that the family come with him and his squires, immediately back to the forest, where his mother lived and died. En route to where Hansel and Gretel were held captive, Hansel asked his sister what proof she might have had, but Gretel only responded that he would see while smiling. This time, it was Gretel's turn to keep a surprising secret from Hansel. Hansel reminded Gretel of their agreement to not hide anything important from each other, but Gretel replied that she would not want to spoil anything, even for her brother.

They approached the charred ruins and the smoke had fully stopped now. Herr Gerhardt Hochberg ordered everyone to dismount, and he also did the same. Hansel and Gretel wished that they would never see this place again, but Gretel at least knew that this would be the last time. Hansel peered at the still-intact stable, with some anger and fear, but then wondered what the stable was like when a horse lived there in the past. Gundovald and Adalberta wished that they could help Hansel and Gretel, but both knew that only the children could help everyone out of this seeming mess. The knight approached the children, but more towards Gretel, and asked for the proof. The squires postulated that nothing could be found in the charred remains, while they looked at each other, shaking their heads and shrugging their shoulders. However, Gretel took the imposing knight by the hand, and led him, with Hansel closely following to this trap door in the ground, where only the hook was visible. She then cleared the deadwood, dirt and rocks, which fully revealed the door. Herr Gerhardt Hochberg, who was already astonished, admitted that he did not know of what appeared to be some extra storage vault of his mother's stead. Then, Gretel forewarned everyone that what they were about to see might disturb them, and opened the door. There was a large underground storage vault, where many dozens of skeletal remains of young children lay. All the bones were picked clean, which easily gave the impression that the numerous children who preceded Hansel and Gretel were cannibalized. Herr Gerhardt Hochberg, Hansel, Gundovald, Adalberta, and the squires in total shock and sadness all quickly kneeled and crossed themselves. Gretel joined the group, while Hansel started feeling a little afraid again, now knowing that he and his sister could have joined those in the storage vault. However, Gretel reached for her brother's hand to reassure him, which worked nicely. The knight recited a prayer for the little souls of the tortured, killed and cannibalized, and that God may take them under His comfort in Heaven. Everyone else prayed with him for this. When everyone stood up again, Gundovald and Adalberta quickly ran to hold Hansel and Gretel again. Herr Gerhardt Hochberg then mentioned that he had no idea whatsoever that his mother was killing and cannibalizing young children with a face as serious as that of Hansel and Gretel in the first encounter of this day. Hansel and Gretel then admitted that the knight's mother was cannibalizing children for her witchcraft practice to keep herself alive longer and to eventually regain her youth. The knight, who knew that his mother was surprisingly living a long life, only answered that he paid his mother weekly visits, bringing her a lot of nourishing foods, which he mentioned was actually what kept her alive, healthy and strong. Herr Gerhardt Hochberg then mentioned that his mother was once a wonderful person and a great mother, and that she raised four children including him. However, she later had volunteered to spend her elder years in the forest, where she would be among nature, despite her son and his siblings refusing her to leave their comforting estate and fiefdom, which once belonged to the knight's father who was also a knight himself and had passed away earlier. Herr Gerhardt Hochberg was also very wealthy and he and his family were among the very few that were only little affected during the famine. Herr Gerhardt Hochberg then said that his mother once had a horse that lived in the stable, but on one of his weekly visits, he caught her in the act of consuming the horse after roasting it, all in the midst of all of his provided food, which made him fear that his mother was becoming crazy, living all alone like this. Yet, Methildis continued to insist that she live within the mountains alone, despite repeated futile efforts to coax her to return to the estate. Then, the knight admitted that when anyone ages, there is always the occasional desire for the unattainable restoration of one's youth, but he did not believe in witchcraft. He quickly mentioned that cannibalizing small children could not accomplish her goals, which everyone, especially Hansel and Gretel, agreed upon. Herr Gerhardt Hochberg closed by saying that if he only knew of this earlier, he would have stopped his mother, and many more children would have been saved from this awful premature death. He knew that famine took its toll on a whole lot of the populace, despite him and his wife doing all to help keep their fiefdom fed. However, death like this was completely deplorable to him. However, as the knight knelt down again, but this time on behalf of his mother feeling sad, he wished that he was more aware that she was gravitating towards crazier and much more sinister acts. Hansel and Gretel joined the knight by placing their hands on his shoulders, and said that they forgave him and took his unawareness with understanding. Herr Gerhardt Hochberg was indeed happy that these young children accepted his apology and understood him at least.

Then, Herr Gerhardt Hochberg approached Gundovald Holzhacker and his fiancé, and offered them along with Hansel and Gretel a home to live on his fiefdom. Gundovald and Adalberta turned their heads to Hansel and Gretel, who looked at each other first, smiling. Then, they both enthusiastically nodded their heads with their father and aunt hoping that they would do so. Gundovald and Adalberta most certainly accepted the offer. Herr Gerhardt Hochberg ordered his squires to escort the Holzhacker family to his estate, where they would be given their new home in much greater comfort. He asked the children about his mother's private stash, and they admitted that they took it only after the house burnt. Technically, the money should pass to the knight and his siblings, but Herr Gerhardt Hochberg turned to Gundovald, Adalberta, Hansel and Gretel and nicely mentioned that they could use the extra help from him. Adalberta approached the knight and kissed him, prior to bowing to him. Gundovald followed with a handshake and a bow to the knight as well. Hansel and Gretel sheepishly grinned and bowed to Herr Gerhardt Hochberg as well. The knight paused for a moment, and then he surprisingly removed his helm and bowed back to them with a reassuring smile. Hansel and Gretel giggled in response. All the squires were also happy that all was well again, and everyone set forth to the fiefdom of Herr Gerhardt Hochberg.

16

It was the summer of 1317, and longer periods of sunny days and warmer weather finally returned to medieval Europe and the Holy Roman Empire of Germany. The famine was finally over, and crops were growing faithfully again, including those grown by Gundovald Holzhacker and his family. Gundovald, Adalberta, Hansel and Gretel enjoyed a wonderful harvest with all others who lived on the knight's fiefdom, and everyone was happy. Gundovald still practiced his trade of woodcutting and obtained his wood from the nearby Harz Mountain forests, but he could finally do it without extreme worry. Gundovald still only obtained chopped wood from dead trees to fell and from recently fallen trees. The family of four had no problem paying a small tribute installment to Herr and Frau Gerhardt Hochberg, who provided protection for all who lived on his fiefdom. The knight's siblings—two noblewomen and another knight—lived on their own fiefdoms, but occasionally paid a visit to Herr Gerhardt Hochberg's fiefdom. Hansel and Gretel liked their new house, which was slightly larger than their old one, but still as simple, which was no problem at all. Their beds were much more comfortable with linen sheets, which they were happy to have for their nightly sleep. The fraternal twins received their morning schooling from their new stepmother Adalberta, and they happily worked with her in the garden and during laundry of the linen and wool garments. Hansel and Gretel often asked their aunt and stepmother about their mother Hiltrude, and she always shared with them the fun and games that the two used to enjoy when she and Adalberta was Hansel and Gretel's age. This was often followed with Hansel and Gretel having the ability to play with other children of their age as well during the afternoons within the fiefdom. The Holzhacker cat also seemed to love its new home as well, and the Holzhackers now had more livestock again too, while their two chickens had more company of their own kind again. The Holzhackers now always had plenty to eat, and they enjoyed their mealtimes either with themselves or with other families on the fiefdom. Herr Gerhardt Hochberg offered the family to dine with him in his estate at times too, which Hansel and Gretel especially welcomed the opportunity. The Holzhacker family enjoyed the occasional festivals, with good food, fun and games to share with all others who lived on Herr Gerhardt Hochberg's fiefdom; and the knight himself performed some ring jousting and mounted archery stunts, which amazed everyone. At home, during evening prayer, Gundovald and Adalberta often had Hansel and Gretel in embrace for they still could have lost the children so easily, not long ago. Hansel and Gretel, the fraternal twin brother and sister would still sometimes become involved with the occasional sibling argument, but they always kept their promise to be there for one another well. This would never be difficult because Hansel and Gretel loved each other as good siblings do. One evening, Gretel told Hansel that they were witch hunters, and perhaps the two will be remembered for this all throughout time, and perhaps people will write stories about them. Hansel truthfully admitted that it was actually Gretel who was the true witch hunter, considering that she delivered the final blow to their captor, but Gretel smiled and said that she definitely could not have done it without her brother's help, which helped him understand that he really was a witch hunter too. Hansel and Gretel embraced each other again following, and of course, both shared the hope that neither of them or anyone else of their age would ever have to undergo anything like what they had gone through again. If that was not enough, it was definitely nice that the famine ended and hunger and disease retreated at last.

There would be brand new challenges for Johannes "Hansel" Holzhacker and his twin sister Margaretha "Gretel" Holzhacker ahead of them, but they would only be healthy challenges, at least for the time being. Hansel and Gretel only looked ahead to their horizons of their lives with optimism.

The End

Made in the USA
Lexington, KY
10 March 2014